THE GOLDEN FEATHER

THE GOLDEN FEATHER

A G Waltons

To order additional copies of this book, contact:
Xlibris
800-056-3182
www.Xlibrispublishing.co.uk
Orders@Xlibrispublishing.co.uk
697021

Amber's Dream

One cold winter night on 28 October 2010, Amber was invited to a Halloween party organised by the company she worked for. It was to take place in a lovely location by the Thames River. That night, Amber made a great impact on her colleagues as they could not recognise her in her outfit. She left the party pretty content as it was a success. When she got home, she realised that Joel, her husband, was not in. She became anxious.

Suddenly Amber appeared in a town. It was dark. She could not recognise where she was. There were old-fashioned cars, people all dressed up in a very conservative fashion, and big houses with tall windows. She did not know where she was or why she was there. It was a cold evening; there was a small park opposite to where she was. She walked towards a bench and sat down. She was feeling confused. 'Where am I? Cannot remember anything,' she said to herself. She was starting to panic. No money, nothing that could lead her somewhere known. It was cold, and she started trembling; she did not have a coat. She was wearing a short black flapper dress showing her attractive legs and a short brown wig with a fringe. In spite of her situation, she looked naturally pretty.

Few people were walking along the park. Amber was too shy and scared to ask questions. She saw a lady passing by, elegantly dressed in the sixties fashion. Amber courteously said, 'Excuse me, madam.' The lady looked at her arrogantly and said coldly, 'Yes.'

'Would you please tell me the name of this town?' Amber asked pleadingly.

She answered, 'Camden Town.' Something came into Amber's mind as if she could recognise the town's name but could not make anything out of it. While walking away and looking at her and her short dress, the lady said insinuatingly, 'You should be heading to the Majestic Club,' and left Amber behind. Amber decided to follow her from a distance and could see an outstanding place, quite crowded. She needed a warm place. One minute more and she could get frozen to death. Even though she was not used to places like that, she went in rapidly.

A handsome man in his forties approached Amber. He was fairly tall, well educated, and formally dressed, with short fair hair, a clean look, brown eyes, and fair skin. He said, 'How do you do? Would you care for a drink? You seem to need it. You are shivering! Please allow me to request a drink for you.'

Amber assented gratefully and said, 'Thanks, I do need it.'

'What would you like to drink?' he asked.

'Gin and tonic will do, thanks.' He went to the bar and got the drinks, then came back and asked her to follow him to a table.

She was not sure about what was happening; she was worried as she still could not figure out where she was or who the gentleman was. He said calmly and politely, 'Please allow me to introduce myself. My name is James. May I know your name?'

She shyly answered, 'I do not know my name.'

He smiled and said, 'I could not blame you for not telling me your name as I am a stranger. I quite understand.'

As Amber was having the first sips of her drink, she started to feel calmer and more relaxed. 'Thanks very much for your kindness, Mr James,' she said warmly.

'No need to call me mister. Please call me James,' he said courteously.

'I honestly do not know my name, James. Can you believe that I am not sure what I am doing here or who I am? No one seems to know me, and I feel terrified,' Amber said worriedly.

'You are quite safe. I shall protect you until we establish your situation. Let's make the most of the evening. I am actually escaping from the pressure of my family, looking for some diversion, and probably you are in the same mood,' James assumed, and Amber did not know what to say.

After a few drinks, Amber was feeling more relaxed and safer. Although she did not know James, his charming and caring ways made her feel more comfortable; nothing undesirable was to happen to her. The club was about to close, so James took off his coat and put it on Amber's back. Then he took her arm gently and asked her to go with him.

When they were walking along the street, James said, 'I have a property nearby. It is my private location where a few of my family and friends can find me. It is a perfect place for you to stay, if you wish.' Amber was unsure, but at the same time, something was telling her to be calm as she felt he was a gentleman.

They took a cab and went to the house. The house was glamorously furnished and with antiques all around. Amber felt enchanted by it. James told her that there were several rooms and she could stay in one of them without a problem. Amber felt relieved as outside was too cold to bear. After a short conversation about James's paintings, he said, 'It would be better for you to retire to your room and have a good sleep. It could help you to remember more in the morning.' He directed her to the guest's bedroom, and before she entered, she said goodnight to him. The room was luxuriously decorated. Amber looked around, experiencing some kind of happiness. A few minutes later, James knocked on the door and handed her towels and one of his bathrobes. Then he wished her goodnight once again and closed the door behind him.

At 7.15 p.m., the telephone rang, and Amber ran to get the phone. 'Hello, darling, are you on your way home?' she asked.

'Yes, you can make my coffee now. I am about twenty minutes from home,' he said. They lived in a maisonette near to Wimbledon Station.

Joel was around ten years older than Amber. He was stocky and very attractive, with thick eyebrows, a charming-looking face, and an unforgettable voice. They had been married for a number of years. They had a good understanding, and most of all, Joel was able to provide Amber with the protection she needed. He was a very talented man who spoke various languages and was a musician. Despite all his good qualities, Joel fell into the gambling world, which took him out of his way.

Once again, Amber found herself in the town, and she could not understand why this was happening again. It was familiar to her. She remembered she had been there before, not exactly when. Amber felt as if someone were there waiting for her, and suddenly James appeared with his warm smile and said, 'How are you, dear?'

Amber replied with a smile, 'Fine, thanks. I do apologise, but have we met before?'

James smiled and said, 'You still cannot remember who you are? I am James. Have you no recollections about me?'

'Well, I am not sure, but your voice seems to be familiar to me. I am still trying to remember without success,' replied Amber.

'I am the one who cannot understand why you disappeared without even saying farewell, my dear lady, but I will let you be,' James said patiently.

'James, I do not understand. It seems as if I am suffering from mental lapses, so sorry! Please forgive me,' Amber said sincerely.

James smiled and said enthusiastically, 'It is delightful to see you again, so while the situation crystallises, we should forget what is happening now. What a lovely evening! As we are near the house, shall I invite you in?'

'That would be lovely, James. Thanks very much. You are very kind and patient with me.'

And he answered warmly, 'That happens when I find a lovely face in need. I am so glad to be of service.'

Amber said, 'You are my only help, and you are like an angel to me.'

They went into the house, and Amber asked him if she could prepare the tea as she wanted to help in some way. 'I would be most grateful! It has been a long time since I was looked after,' James said, pleased. They went to the lounge.

While having their tea, James asked Amber, 'Have you not remembered your name yet?'

Amber responded, 'I am afraid not. I even do not know what I am doing here.'

'Do not be worried. I will need to give you a name. Tell me, what name would you like until you remember yours?'

'Not sure. You could choose it as you are my protector,' Amber said.

'Very well, shall I call you Rose?' James asked.

Amber looked at him, assenting, and said, 'It is a beautiful name. I like it very much.'

James said, 'I am glad you like it, Rose. By the way, my sister, Loren, left some clothes behind in a wardrobe in one of the rooms, and you are welcome to wear them as I am sure my sister would not mind. Loren used to visit me a lot, but now she seems to have forgotten me. Rose, my dear, would you wear one of Loren's nightdresses? I have two theatre tickets, and I would love you to accompany me.'

Rose was getting used to his calm ways and felt so much at home that without hesitation, she answered, 'That's a great idea. I would be very pleased to go with you, but I need to know something about you before going ahead.'

'Yes, what is it?' asked James eagerly.

'Are you in a relationship, or is there anybody special? Because I do not want to cause any problems or disturb your life,' said Rose.

'Please relax, dear. I am a bachelor and have no involvement with any lady in particular, so I am free like a bird. Please do not preoccupy yourself. As you cannot recollect about your life yet, if any person addresses you, I would rather you allow me to engage in the conversation to prevent uncomfortable enquiries, is that all right?'

'Yes, it is fine. Now I am going to change and won't be long. I will check your sister's wardrobe, see what I can find,' Rose answered relaxedly.

After an hour, Rose came out of the bedroom with a lovely long light-green dress and said, 'I find the fashion unusual for whatever reason but still very comfortable and lovely. How do I look?'

'Well, honestly?' James asked.

'Yes, James, please be honest!' said Rose.

'You look beautiful, and I could not be more proud.'

'Thanks, James,' Rose answered, very pleased.

'The theatre starts at 8 p.m., so we still have a couple of hours to spare. Would you care for a drink, Rose?'

'Yes, please, James, and we are to talk about you as I have nothing to tell about myself,' said Rose amusingly.

'Very well, I will tell you all about me, but you will need to try to remember. And if you disappear again, my dear, you will need to remember me and our place of meeting.'

'I will do, James,' said Rose.

James told her about his family, who lived in Surrey Manor, two hours from the town. His parents were Mr and Mrs Gobbling; he had a sister called Loren and a brother called Jeffrey.

At that time, Mr and Mrs Gobbling, Jeffrey, and Loren were in Florence, visiting friends. Mr and Mrs Gobbling were very worried about Loren's status, and the fact that she had not been taking life seriously demanded their attention as society played a major role in their lives. They needed to get her married to someone wealthy in their society.

Loren was a beautiful English flower in her twenties, with slim figure and long fair hair. There was no doubt she would get someone's attention very soon. Jeffrey was a handsome, tall, elegant young man and was already engaged to a wealthy lady. Luckily for Rose, James was independent, old enough to know what he wanted out of life, and he was still a bachelor.

Once again, Amber was with her husband, Joel. She felt strangely happy and loved. Her husband looked at her and gave her a cuddle. She was feeling more cheerful and energetic, but she could not understand the change of scenery. They were planning their Christmas dinner as it was their custom to cook together, have a drink, play cards, and watch TV.

As usual, Joel would prepare roast lamb. Amber was in charge of the shopping. She was to make sure all the ingredients were to be bought as the supermarkets would be closed for the festivities. Christmas Day was a relaxing day, and they were off work. They cooked and enjoyed their meal and the evening. Amber looked at Joel's unusual ring and asked him to tell her the story about it and the especial box he had given her as a tenth wedding anniversary present. Joel told her that on one of his trips a few years ago, he went to Egypt to meet up with some musicians. He thought he needed a very special present to symbolise his love for Amber. One day, he walked through Cairo's market for about an hour, looking for something unusual, something that could call his attention. Suddenly he saw an old man with some dusty objects placed on a table. His stall was not a very visible one, so Joel greeted him and said respectfully, 'Dear sir, do you realise that your stall is kind of hidden and that will not help you to do business?'

The old man responded, 'Dear friend, I am not here for business like the others. What I sell is quite particular, and only certain people are expected to see my stall and especial items.'

Joel asked him curiously, 'Do you mean that I was expected today?'

'Yes, sir,' responded the old man.

'Interesting. If that is the case, please show me the merchandise, and I will see if there is anything that can interest me,' Joel said enthusiastically.

'You are to choose three objects, sir,' said the old man.

'Well, I assume it will be what my pocket can afford, my old friend,' said Joel, intrigued. The old man kept quiet and waited. Joel started looking, and he could see a very unusual ring. He asked for the price, and the old man said to him, 'Dear friend, keep on looking, and once you have the three objects, we can negotiate a price.'

'Okay, sir,' said Joel. Then he saw a feather bookmark, quite unusual too. The third object that enchanted Joel was a lovely wooden box with a symbol of a bird engraved on it, very colourful and appealing. 'I do not see any other objects that can be of interest. Now, sir, please give me the price, and I hope I can afford them.'

'How much money do you have?' enquired the old man.

Joel was a man who loved bargains and was a very assertive man too. Although he had some money on him, he only offered twenty Egyptian pounds. The old man did not argue the price and accepted the offer. This unexpected action called Joel's attention as normally there were long negotiations among the traders and customers. Joel decided to give him fifty pounds as he knew they looked like expensive objects and he did not want to be unfair. The old man said, 'I thank you for your generosity, and please treasure these objects as they are priceless. I accept the money, but their value is more spiritual than commercial.'

'It has been a pleasure doing business with you, sir,' said Joel.

'It has been a pleasure for me too. These objects are meant for the owners. God is with you, sir,' said the old man with satisfaction.

Joel finished telling the story and said to Amber, 'The following day, I took a friend to the market and looked for the old man and his stall, but we could not find a trace of him or his stall, and no one seemed to know about him. That was so weird! I kept the puzzle ring for myself and gave you the other two presents as per our wedding anniversary, remember, darling?'

Amber cuddled and kissed him and said, 'Thank you, darling. What a lovely story! I love you.'

And Joel said proudly, 'That was a token of my great love for you. I love you, my darling,' and kissed her tenderly.

Amber felt there was some kind of magic about the story and the objects. She remembered the day when she opened the box for the first time. She was enchanted by the feather bookmark; it was very unusual. She could not guess what bird the feather came from. It had lovely colours, but it was not from a peacock. It was so fine and soft. It shone beautifully in the darkness. The wooden box was as beautiful. It had a colourful bird engraved that turned golden at night, and both of the presents gave her a kind of inner peace, happiness, and tranquillity.

Amber decided to keep the box containing the feather on her bedside table so she could contemplate it any time she wanted. Moreover, the only two people in the house were Joel and her, so there was no chance of losing it in any way.

Joel could be, at times, a very jealous and possessive character. Sometimes he noticed Amber so happy that it made him think that she could be having an affair or she was into something he did not know. He kept waiting for a good opportunity to talk about it.

Amber used to go to her work early in the morning and go home in the evening. She worked in an office surrounded by native English speakers and some Europeans. She was the only one from South America. London, as a multicultural city, had people from different backgrounds, and most of them were born in the UK. It was difficult to identify if the persons were either of English or mixed backgrounds. Amber's accent was her signature, and she was proud of it. She was the type of person who loved being different.

Mr and Mrs Grajales, Amber's parents, educated themselves on extensive reading, in spite of not having had the opportunity of attending school in their time. They brought their children up with moral values. They taught them to treat everyone equally, and family ties were very important. That was the reason why Amber's favourite film was *A Christmas Carol* as it was a film with a moral on human behaviour and fate.

Moreover, as the Grajales family lived in a Catholic environment, the children were taught to be open and respectful to other beliefs as life's mysteries were to be respected. They were also taught be grateful for each minute of life as if it were the last. Forgiveness and understanding were very important in their lives.

Once again, Rose appeared in the park, and who was there waiting? James—he was showing a big smile.

'Rose!' he called, and Rose was so happy to see him. She could remember him. 'James, I remember you! I do hope I can keep on remembering everything,' she enthusiastically said.

He held her hand and said, 'Please, let me take you home. Have you recalled any more about yourself?'

'I am afraid not.'

'That is fine. I wish to make a personal remark. I hope not to cause you any uneasiness,' James said.

'That's fine, James. What is it?' she asked.

He looked into her eyes and said, 'I am in the habit of being with you, and I would love you not to disappear any more, if possible. Also, I would love us to remain like this—you and I, no past, only the present. But I assume it is too perfect, is it not?'

'James, let's live in the present as it is. What we have now might change. We do not know what is in store for us,' said Rose.

'I quite agree, Rose. We will live in the present only. By the way, we did not go to the theatre last time.'

'Oh, James, I am so sorry, but what happened?'

'You disappeared, my dear, and I kept on waiting in the park every evening at the usual time, checking if you were to appear again, and yes! Today is a fortunate day!' he said happily.

'Let's go home and have something to eat before you disappear again,' said James.

'How embarrassing! Please forgive me!' said Rose regretfully.

Rose was wondering how she could disappear from one place to another without knowing what was happening. She had to find out what was going on. She decided to enjoy James's company as she was falling in love with him and his gentle ways.

James said, 'Rose, I would need to hire an investigator to obtain information about you. Someone might be looking for you. It is quite a mysterious and delicate situation.'

Rose replied, 'I do agree with you, James. But I hope we can find out information without getting into trouble with anybody.'

'That is true. We have to be careful as women are getting some kind of freedom nowadays, but it is still in a very early stage. My parents look after my sister like guardians looking after a treasure, and you might have—or certainly have—someone really worried about you. I will ask a friend to discreetly investigate if the police are looking for you. I will let you know if Sergeant Rhodes finds some information. Would you please make some tea which is the best I have ever tasted, even compared to my mother's?' said James.

Rose gave thanks to him and went to make it. While having their tea, Rose asked James, 'How long since you saw me the first time, James?'

'It has been a few months now. You come and go, and then I wait and wait. I promised not to give up waiting for you. Sometimes the thought of knowing that you might be married and have children disturbs me bitterly. I have no desire to lose you. You have brought light into my life.' And he tenderly took her hand and kissed it.

'Dear James, you make me feel so relaxed as if I have known you all my life. Isn't it so strangely beautiful? I also feel afraid of finding out, what if I am married with children and if by remembering I am going to lose you? I have very confused feelings. Shall we talk about something else, please, if you do not mind?' Rose said worriedly.

'Of course, my dear Rose, let's talk about the theatre. There are always new plays to enjoy,' he said happily.

The following day, James went to his office. He was the director of his own company. His clothing business was in progress, so he needed to pass by and check how everything was going inside the factory.

The doorbell rang at James's house, and this was a new, unexpected experience for Rose. She decided to open the door; a tall, slim man was out there. He asked for James, and Rose said what she knew. The man looked at her curiously and asked, 'I hope you do not mind me asking if you are James's relative.' Rose said confidently, 'Yes, I am,' without clarifying what sort of relationship she had with James. She told him that she was rather busy, so she kindly asked him to leave. The man raised his hat as a gesture of courtesy as he said, 'Have a good day, madam,' and left.

Rose was severely distressed, thinking aloud, 'What if that gentleman was James's investigator? I should have asked for his name. How stupid of me! James is not going to like this.' She was panicking.

'Amber, where are my work shirts? You have not ironed them yet. Waiting for me to ask again?' said Joel angrily.

'Sorry, darling, I am going to do it tonight, I promise,' said Amber, distressed. She did not want to argue with Joel. He was always right.

Once again, Rose appeared in the park, and James was waiting for her. 'My dear Rose, how delightful to see you,' James eagerly said.

And Rose responded tenderly, 'Hello, dear James.'

'When I returned home, you were gone—you, my sweet little thing.' James took her hand, and they walked hand in hand, enjoying the promenade. 'This time, I have no wish to leave you alone, and I trust you shall not disappear.' said James happily.

They went into the house. In the lounge area, there was a beautiful Victorian fireplace situated in the middle of the room. There were four oil paintings of the sequence of sea waves hanging on the walls and two comfortable antique armchairs, which they used to sit and talk.

'Rose, it is such a pleasure to have you around,' said James sitting by her side. The sitting room was an enchanting place for Rose.

Rose answered sweetly, looking at James, 'I love seeing you. You make me feel safe and welcome, and this house is so lovely and enchanting.' She gave him a kiss on the cheek, and as they kept on looking into each other's eyes, their lips joined in a passionate and sweet kiss.

'I desire you to stay with me. I need you, Rose!' said James in a pleading way.

Rose looked warmly at him. 'I do not want to be away from you, but if I do, you know I will always be back and look for you. I remembered something, James,' Rose said excitedly.

'What is it, my dear?' he asked curiously.

'On my previous visit, when I was alone in the house, waiting for you, a gentleman came to see you. He did not leave his name, and I felt very stupid for not asking for his details,' said Rose.

'Darling, I was expecting the investigator, Mr Darlington. He is tall and heavyset. He is a man of few words. Did he leave any message?' asked James.

'No, he only asked me if I was a relative, and he certainly does not fit your description,' said Rose, very preoccupied.

'Oh no, I have no knowledge about the gentleman in question. The investigator would have left a message for me and would have made no enquiries about you or our relationship as such information would have been provided. Do not be preoccupied, my darling. That gentleman will not dare to show himself again,' said James confidently. 'Rose, in regard to your situation, before you vanish . . .'

'What is it, James?' Rose asked.

'You appear to vanish when you face distressful moments.'

'Is that true, James? So you think that if I try not to panic, I might be able to control it and not disappear?'

'It is possible, my love. I should be more observant about your behaviour, especially when troubled. Darling, it is my wish to know where you go when you disappear and to be able to follow you,' said James hopefully.

Rose worriedly said, 'I wish to know too so I can be more in control of this strange situation.'

The following day, Rose got up and went to the kitchen to make breakfast while James went to his study to check his post. James received a letter from the investigator, and it read, 'I, Mr Darlington, confirm that it was completely impossible and out of my hands to obtain any information about Ms Rose. The available sources have no information or file about the mentioned lady. Therefore, I am bound to close the investigation, expecting your response in return.'

James folded the letter and decided not to tell Rose. He thought the news was of no use, and it could cause her more distress. He did not want to incur any suffering to his darling Rose.

When they were having dinner, Rose said to James, 'I see that some of the ladies walking on the street seem very conservative, and the ones we saw in the club were dressed up in a more liberated way as I was dressed the first time you saw me.'

'Yes,' James responded. 'The new fashion means women independence from social conventions. I understand women as they have been facing changes and wars. They have become stronger, more aware of what they want. I personally quite like it, but part of the society does not like the change. As you can see, the conservative fashion is still here, but the new fashion is having an impact on the society. It is quite interesting! Well, dear, I am afraid I have some business to attend to, so I should go. I would rather stay with you, but it is not possible.' James kissed Rose softly and promised not to be long.

Fifteen minutes later, there was a knock on the door. Rose was in shock. She did not know whether to open the door or not. She got herself together and opened the door. A lady was there, looking surprised, but she gently spoke, 'How do you do? Is my brother home? May I enter?'

'Yes, sure, please come in. You must be Ms Loren,' said Rose excitedly.

Loren entered and said softly, 'I beg your pardon, have we met?' feeling confused as she had said her name without being introduced.

Rose said, 'Oh no, you do not know me. James has spoken about you so much.'

'Well, my dear brother has been talking about me. May I know who you are, please?' Loren asked gently.

Rose did not want to say much and said, 'I am a friend of your brother.'

'And are you staying with my brother? I guess, as he is so independent, he kept the secret from me,' said Loren jestingly.

'Loren, please! I do not want to get him into trouble, and I would appreciate if you could keep this between us. James loves you, and I am sure he would have trusted you in regard to my presence,' Rose said imploringly.

Loren smiled pleasantly and said, 'Please do not be distressed. Certainly, I shall keep the secret. That is not a problem, but my brother should explain to me in detail what is going on. I love him to bits, and we are quite close. It will be taken as a confidential matter. We are to be friends, so I will start by saying please feel free to wear my clothes or anything you might need.' She looked at Rose wearing one of her bathrobes.

'I am already wearing your bathrobe. Please forgive me!' said Rose, embarrassed.

'I have nothing to forgive, my dear. What is your name, if I may know?'

'Please accept my apologies. My name is Rose.'

'Lovely name, Rose. My brother is taking too long, and I came just for a few minutes. Would you please let him know that I came around and that I will come back next week?' Loren said in haste.

Rose said with a smile, 'I will certainly let James know that you came to see him, and I will pass on your message.'

'Much obliged, Rose. You are very sweet, and I cannot expect less of my brother's friends. I like you, and it has been a pleasure to have made your acquaintance. Have a good afternoon.'

Loren kissed Rose on the cheek and left merrily. Rose closed the door and felt very happy as this time it was a more pleasant visitor. *I hope I am not causing problems to James*, she thought.

James came back home, and Rose ran to greet him, 'Oh, James, I missed you so much, my darling!'

'Rose, darling, I was longing to come back home! I had the thought you might have probably vanished, but to my good fortune, you are here.' He could not stop kissing her softly as if it were the last time he would see her.

'I have a message to give you,' Rose said.

'What is it, my darling?' he asked.

'Your sister, Loren, came to see you this afternoon.'

'What a delightful surprise!' James said, pleased. 'Oh, my dear love, poor you, I expect it was an amiable encounter as Loren is a sweet-natured girl.'

'Oh yes, she was a very sweet darling. She offered me her clothes and belongings, the kindest and sweetest person apart from you that I have encountered,' said Rose pleasantly.

'Oh, darling, I should speak to Loren about you. We want our relationship to be kept confidential as per the circumstances,' said James anxiously.

'Do not worry, darling,' Rose said. 'I have already asked her kindly to do so, and she has agreed to keep our secret.'

'Marvellous! It pleases me greatly to know that we complement each other. I love you and need you,' James said warmly.

'Darling, you are my soul mate,' said Rose, and they finished the conversation with a kiss.

The telephone rang, and James answered. 'Hello, 1456. How may I help you?' There was a feminine voice at the other end. 'Darling James, you have me abandoned. What is the matter? You have not called me nor visited me. I have to complain about it. What is the matter, dear?'

'Dear Louise, how do you do?' asked James calmly.

'I am very well but missing you dearly,' said Louise, insinuating.

James was trying to cut the conversation short so Amber would not be stressed. 'I am awfully sorry. I promise I will call you another day as I am rather occupied at the moment. Please forgive me, dear,' said James politely.

Louise said disappointedly and angrily, 'I take your promise, and I will be expecting your call soon. I demand an explanation. I won't hold you any longer. Have a good afternoon, dear James.'

James responded rapidly, 'Have a good afternoon, Louise,' and he hung up.

Rose approached him sweetly and said, 'Was that Louise again, darling?'

James was taken by surprise and answered, 'Yes, darling. How do you know?'

Rose said, 'She phoned an hour ago, and I did tell her you were to be home soon. She had the impression that I was your maid, and I let her believe that. She did mention my accent, and although she spoke to me and I understood every single word she said, I could tell that she was not satisfied as I could hear when she made a comment to someone else near her, "James has a foreign maid who can hardly speak the language." I did not pay attention to her comment.'

James, embracing Rose, said, 'I must agree with you, my darling. Louise's attitude towards us is not worth of our attention.' They both laughed.

The night came, and they were having a glass of wine, sitting by the fireplace. They were like a pair of lovebirds wanting to have the silence as their friend. Their eyes could talk more than words could say. At the end of the evening, James accompanied Rose to her room, wishing her goodnight.

A few days later, the doorbell rang, and Rose was very agitated. It sounded as if someone was going to break the door. She heard a shouting voice, 'Come down, maid. Open the door, I know you are in!'

'Amber, where are my reading glasses?' her husband asked sternly. Amber went to the bedroom and got them. 'Here they are, darling,' said Amber, smiling.

'Thank you, darling. By the way, there is going to be an interesting programme on BBC One tonight. David Attenborough will be presenting a nature documentary, and I would like you to watch it with me. I know it is one of your favourite programmes,' Joel said.

'Okay, darling, I will do the washing-up and make the coffees so we can watch it from the beginning,' said Amber enthusiastically. Discussing life, documentaries, and books and singing together were common interests between them. Amber only wished her husband would be better with the money. Religion was not an issue as they came to a conclusion that all religions follow the same God.

The following day, Amber went to Oxford Street to do some shopping. She bought a cheap new black top and a short black skirt to be worn with leggings. Although she was not in her twenties, she looked very young. When she got home, she went to the bathroom, lit the candles all around the bath, put the soft music on, and enjoyed the long, relaxing bath. Suddenly she was disturbed by the phone ringing, and it was Joel letting her know that he was on his way home. Amber continued getting ready. It was going to be New Year's Eve. She was struggling with her feelings, but she was trying not to show it to Joel as she wanted to have a pleasant evening.

When Joel came home, he noticed Amber's new outfit and asked, 'Is that a new outfit, what you got on? It looks good on you, but you are not a spring chicken any more.' They both laughed. She said, 'But I feel young,' and Joel replied, 'You are just as young as you feel, my dear.'

'Darling, I am glad you managed to get the day off for us to celebrate New Year together,' said Amber, and Joel agreed. When midnight came, Amber felt sad. She used to celebrate New Year surrounded by her family, so that made her feel homesick. They watched the fireworks on TV, then she realised Joel was fast asleep on the sofa.

Rose appeared in the park again, longing to see James. James was there waiting for her. She ran to him, and they both embraced tightly. 'Oh, James, oh, darling,' Rose said, bursting into tears.

'Oh, my darling Rose, it seems to be a long time since I last saw you. I desired strongly to see you,' said James.

'Embrace me, darling, very tightly. Please, I need you,' said Rose.

James kept her in his arms and let her cry. 'I am here for you, my darling, and I will always be. Remember this,' he said sweetly.

'Oh, James, dear, I think I am starting to remember things, and I . . .' She could not continue. He embraced her and said, 'Say no words, my darling. Let's go home.' Rose felt the love and peace that she was longing for.

'James, I am going to tell you something, but please promise me you are not to change your feelings towards me. I am so afraid,' she said, crying.

James said, 'Calm down, my darling. We shall have a drink first, and then you can tell me what is disturbing you. My feelings for you will be eternal, darling, so do not be worried. Whatever is the matter, a solution can be found.'

Rose had a sip of her drink and said, 'I think that I am married, darling, and I am not sure if I am doing something wrong by being with you.' She sobbed.

James was shocked by the news but calmly said, 'It is only a faint recollection, darling.'

Rose said sweetly, 'Can we please continue talking about it tomorrow? I just want to have a lovely evening with you in our way. Can we?'

'Yes, darling, we shall talk in the morning.' They went to her room, lay down together, and had a short conversation before they both fell asleep.

Few days later, Amber appeared on a train on her way to work. She was reading a classic of English literature, her favourite novel, *Wuthering Heights*. She had seen the film when she was young, and since then, she had loved the story. Sometimes, she used to miss the station where she was to get off as she was so much into the book, thinking she was the main character and feeling such love between Cathy and Heathcliff.

Once again, Rose was in the park, and James was waiting for her. 'Rose!' he called. Rose ran to him. 'Oh, James darling, how many days have I been away from you?' said Rose, preoccupied.

'A few days,' said James, 'but not to be worried about it, darling. Predicting your appearances has become somehow easier for me. If I were not here, would you remember where to find me?'

'Yes,' she said softly and relaxed. 'I know where your house is.'

'My life has changed since I met you, and home is now the best place to be, especially when I have you with me. Sometimes I have the thought of being selfish, and I have no wish to know about your past or real present as my happiness is you and our present,' James said.

Rose looked at him pensively and then said, 'I feel scared of remembering more about my life as I do not want to lose you. I also think that it is better to stay as we are. Has your investigator found out anything?'

And James answered, 'I am afraid nothing yet. You have no one trying to find you, as far as we know, here in England. You have a lovely accent, but it does not tell us much as we have people from all around the world in this country. Let's go home, darling.' They held hands and walked away.

Meanwhile in another part of England, James's mother had a visitor—a tall, slim, elegant woman with long dark hair called Louise. 'Dear Ms Louise Lobberby, how delightful to see you again. I received your letter requesting to see me. Come in, dear, let's have tea first.' Mrs Gobbling called the maids to serve the tea. Once they were left alone, Louise Lobberby whispered to Mrs Gobbling, 'Mrs Gobbling, I am very preoccupied about James.'

'And why are you worried about him, my dear?' asked Mrs Gobbling.

'Well, has he contacted you as often as he used to?' asked Louise.

'Well, my dear, we have been away, so I cannot comment on that.'

'Well, Mrs Gobbling, he used to phone me very regularly. But for the last few months, I have noticed that he does not attempt to visit me as before, and I happened to have passed by his property in London and . . .' She stopped talking, and Mrs Gobbling became very curious. 'Dear Miss Lobberby, if you do not tell me soon, I am going to have a heart attack. What is the matter with James?'

Louise answered, 'Mrs Gobbling, he has a woman in his house. Did you know that?'

'Good Lord!' said Mrs Gobbling, surprised by the news. 'It cannot be true. He has never told me anything about it, and moreover, women that belong to aristocratic families like ours would never create such a situation. Who is this woman?'

'I believe she is a maid, but I am not sure,' answered Louise.

'Oh, dear Ms Lobberby, James does need maids in the house. I am glad he has finally listened to me as I do not want him struggling with the house duties. Relax, Ms Lobberby, it was an issue that was worrying me, but now I feel better. There will be a person serving my dear son,' said Mrs Gobbling happily.

Louise said to Mrs Gobbling, 'So it was your idea, Mrs Gobbling?'

'Yes, dear, please do not be worried about it. By the way, have you been invited to Mr and Mrs Grobble's ball?' asked Mrs Gobbling.

'Oh yes! I am looking forward to the ball. You know, it is an opportunity to find suitable husbands. Is James coming to the ball?' asked Louise eagerly.

'Yes, my dear, a ball is never to be missed by James as he loves amusing himself. There will be a large number of ladies after my James—a bachelor with a fortune of a hundred thousand a year and a handsome gentleman. What else could a lady desire, Louise?' said Mrs Gobbling proudly of her son James.

'I should look forward to having the first dance with James,' said Louise impatiently.

The ball was to happen the following Saturday, and James was with Rose in his house. The telephone rang, and James answered it. 'Mother, how lovely to hear from you,' he said sweetly. 'I am awfully sorry, but I cannot attend Mr and Mrs Grobble's ball. I feel unwell. I shall not fail the next ball invitation.'

'What on earth are you saying, son? Are you ill? Do you need a doctor?' his mother anxiously enquired.

'No, Mother, I have no need for a doctor. Please do not be preoccupied, and accept my apologies, Mother. I promise I shall visit you very soon.' James was in haste to hang up, but his mother kept on talking.

'Dear son, you will be missed, but I guess nothing can be done. Do take care of yourself. I hope your maid will be there to look after you,' said Mrs Gobbling.

James was surprised to hear about the maid, but he decided to disregard his mother's comments and said, 'See you soon, Mother. Do have a good afternoon.' James hung up the telephone. Rose came and embraced him.

James said to Rose, 'It is a pleasure to have an excuse not to have to attend a ball. An advantageous marriage is all that is in my mother's mind and the aristocratic society we belong to.' Then he whispered into Rose's ear, 'I have not considered marriage until I met you, darling Rose.'

'Darling, you know I still do not know much about myself, and your family may not accept me for who I am,' said Rose.

'Well, you are the lady I have chosen to make an offer in marriage, and we can face society together,' said James,

Rose kissed him tenderly. 'I love you, darling. You are my dearest. I feel so happy to hear you say those words. Although I am not sure if I could ever be your wife. I do hope so,' she said dubiously.

Mrs Gobbling had received a letter from Louise requesting to see her urgently. And Mrs Gobbling replied, asking her to come and see her whenever she could as per the urgency of the matter. Two days later, Louise came to Surrey Manor.

'Dear Mrs Gobbling, how delightful to see you,' said Louise.

'Oh, dear Louise, pray come and sit down. I have asked for the tea service already, so no one is to disturb us. I have to tell you the truth—I am extremely curious and immensely worried about your news.'

'Well, Mrs Gobbling, please forgive me for causing you all this suffering, but I trust it is as important for you as it is for me. First of all, please tell me, have you had any news about James?' Louise asked.

'The usual news—that he is fine and that he is too busy to arrange a visit, but he will do his best to make it happen,' said Mrs Gobbling.

'So you have no knowledge about James's actions,' Louise said, triggering Mrs Gobbling's curiosity.

'Good Lord! Louise? Pray speak, Louise,' Mrs Gobbling said impatiently.

'Mrs Gobbling, I have ventured to visit James when I was in London in my last trip. I disguised myself of a man wearing a hat and sunglasses, and when I knocked on his house door, a woman opened it. I am not sure if she is his maid, but she was not wearing an apron. She was polite but did not behave as a maid. Do you know anything about this woman? As I did not perceive her as a lady,' Louise said.

Mrs Gobbling was in complete shock and asked, 'Do you think that James has married this woman without telling us?'

'I do hope that is not the case,' said Louise. 'Mrs Gobbling, I had hopes of marrying James as we knew each other since we were children, and even my father is trying to arrange a meeting with Mr Gobbling to talk about it. He knows I love James dearly.'

'Really, Louise? This is delightful news to me—I did not know that you have strong feelings for my son. I should speak to Mr Gobbling about it as I am now not certain about James,' said Mrs Gobbling.

'This is the reason I am so preoccupied by this woman who is in James's house. Can you understand me now, Mrs Gobbling?'

'Yes, my dear, such situation is going to cause me grief. James is so obstinate sometimes, as much as he is adorable as a son. Dear Louise, I am really trifled about this matter. I am sure James will have an explanation for it. I should ask Mr Gobbling to write to James to request him a private audience as soon as possible,' said Mrs Gobbling agitatedly.

Louise thought that the measures she had taken to tell James's news to his mother would secure her a place in the family so that an offer of marriage was to be made by James. James's mother always showed her liking for Louise, so the only one to convince was the father. Louise adored him like an uncle, but James's father always ended up following his favourite son's ideas.

Louise decided to follow James wherever he went. She started to notice that he walked to the park and sat down on the same bench every single day and stayed there for hours. She did not know he was waiting for Rose. One day James did not go to the park at the usual time due to problems in the factory that required his attention, and that day, Rose turned up in the park. She was surprised not to see James, but instead, a woman was waiting for her. Louise ran to her and said, 'How do you do? I am afraid James could not come today as he has some matters to attend to, so he sent me instead. May I introduce myself? My name is Louise.' Rose was completely speechless and puzzled; in spite of her surprise, she tried to keep calm.

'I assume you were going to James's house, weren't you? Shall we go together?' asked Louise.

Rose was still in shock. She did not want Louise to know about her and her whereabouts, so she responded, 'No, I am not going to James's house. I came to the park as it is quite warm and beautiful out here.'

'It is fine by me if we remain here,' said Louise.

'Please, Louise, do not feel obliged to stay with me,' Rose pleaded.

'Not to worry, my dear. I just want to have a conversation with you, would you mind?'

'I do not mind, but what can we talk about if we don't know each other?' said Rose, trying to be composed.

'Please, dear, I have some questions to ask you. What is your name?'

Rose knew that she was after information. 'My name is Rose, what else do you want to know, Louise?'

'Well, may I know what your relationship with James, my fiancé, is?'

Rose was completely astonished; she thought, *How come James did not tell me about this?* Then she said to Louise calmly but sharply, 'Well, I cannot answer that question. Please try another one.'

'Well, where is your family? Where do you come from?'

'I cannot answer those questions either.'

Louise started feeling angry and frustrated. 'Dear Rose, is there anything you wish to share with me? It seems all my questions are unanswerable,' said Louise sarcastically, feeling agitated.

Suddenly James turned up and said, 'Good afternoon, ladies. How delightful to see you. Louise, it is rather unusual to see you in town. May I know what brought you here?'

She shyly said, 'Oh James! I was just passing by and happened to see Rose and was keeping her company, that is all.'

James said, 'I do hope Rose did not answer your questions, whatever they were.'

Louise said abruptly, 'What is this, James! Are you against me? Have you forgotten that we are engaged to marry?'

James smiled and said, 'My dear Louise, you are like a sister to me, and if there has been any agreement about marriage, I have no knowledge about it. I have no plans to marry you. Would you please excuse us as we need to go.'

Louise was feeling uneasy and in rage, trying to control her feelings, and said, 'Have a good afternoon,' and left hurriedly.

As Rose and James walked along the bridge in Camden Town, James tenderly said, 'Rose, would you care for some tea?'

She said happily, 'Yes, it is a great idea,' so they walked to the house, which was near to the underground station.

They got home, and James approached Rose and cuddled her. He said, 'My darling Rose, please do not pay attention to what Louise said. She has always been after me since childhood, but she cannot accept the fact that I have no desire to marry her. The only person I would marry is you and no one else.' Rose could not help thinking about Louise's words.

Miriam came to visit Amber. She was in her forties, short, with a good figure, fair skin, straight brown hair, small waist, and rather plump legs; she dressed smartly. Amber and Miriam met on a bus stop ten years ago, and they stayed very good friends. She was her best friend since she arrived in London. She belonged to a rich family back in her country; therefore, she had good manners, and money was not a problem for her. 'Dear Miriam, it is such a pleasure to see you. Please do come and have a cup of coffee with me,' Amber said pleasantly. Miriam was so happy to see Amber too.

'Tell me about you, Miriam. Have you had any news from your family?' asked Amber.

'Yes, my brothers and sisters want to sell one of the family properties. Apparently, the rebels in that area are asking for money, and we have already lost a brother who did not agree to support them. I feel sad about the selling, but there is nothing I can do,' she said hopelessly.

'I am sorry to hear about it,' said Amber sincerely.

'Anyway, since my parents died, I promised myself to live my life away from home. I feel safer here, so I will send them a document authorising them to sell my part, and they can do whatever they want with it. When my dad and mum died, I realised that we do not take anything with us to our graves.'

'Well, my dear, you came to the right place at the right time as I would not know what I would do without your friendship. You are my best friend, and I do appreciate you as a sister,' Amber said.

'Amber, you are my best friend and sister too.' They looked at each other with a smile.

'We are to look after each other,' said Miriam.

'Yes,' confirmed Amber.

Miriam seriously said to Amber, 'I have something to tell you, Amber.'

'What is it?' Amber enquired.

'I am leaving my husband. I found his behaviour out of order. I have made the decision.'

'Oh dear, that is a hard decision to make, and I hope it is the right one. And your son? Is he going to be fine?' asked Amber.

'I have to do it for him. I cannot have his father showing such terrible behaviour, and I had enough.'

Amber thought about her own situation and became pensive.

Rose turned up in the park again. Even though it was very cold and quite late in the evening, her beloved James was waiting for her. He approached her and said, 'It is such a relief to see you, my dear. How are you?'

'Oh, darling! I cannot avoid disappearing. I just do not know how it happens,' Rose said, perplexed.

'Perhaps we should request a doctor's advice about your situation,' James said.

'Darling, please let's wait,' Rose said imploringly.

'Why should it be postponed, Rose?' James said desperately.

'Darling, I am going to find out by myself as I seem to be recollecting. Trust me, please.' She sounded determined.

'Very well, I shall wait for you to find out what is happening. A stable life with you is what I desire, Rose. You know I want you near me forever.' He embraced her, and they continued walking towards the house. Once in the house, James took Rose by the hand to her bedroom. She went to her bed, and he tucked her in. Rose asked him to keep her company for a while, so he lay on the bed with her until she fell asleep.

In the morning, he came to the bedroom and kissed her. He left her a note saying that he had to be at his clothing company, and a drawing of a heart was part of his signature. She got up, read the note, and smiled, feeling loved. She started to tidy up the house until she heard a knock on the door. Her heart started palpitating so hard that she thought it was going to get out of her body. She opened the door, and a police sergeant spoke gently, 'Good morning, madam.'

'Good morning, Officer. How may I help?' she asked, trying to calm herself.

'Well, madam, we are from the UK immigration department. My name is Sergeant Smith, and we need to ask you some questions if possible,' said the sergeant.

'May I know what is it about?' she asked anxiously.

'We have been informed that a woman who is an illegal immigrant is living in this house.'

Rose could not talk; she was struck by what she heard as she could not explain to him what was happening. 'I guess I am the person in question. I need to explain, but it is still difficult,' Rose said shakily.

'I am afraid you will need to come with us to the police station.'

'Please allow me to grab my coat,' Rose said. While she was looking for it, she wrote a note to James: 'Dear love, the police came to look for me. I will be at Camden's police station. Lots of love, Rose.'

She quietly got in the police car, and as she was so calm, the police were polite with her.

At the police station, she was asked questions like where she was from, and she told them she did not know. They requested her to provide any documents that could help them to identify her. She told them that she did not have any documents with her, so they asked her whom she did know that could help them as it was an extraordinary situation and needed to be investigated. She told them about James and that he would be around soon as she had left a message.

James arrived home and happily started calling Rose's name, but there was no answer. His first thought was that she had disappeared once again. When he went to the kitchen, he saw a note over the kitchen worktop and read it. He rapidly put his coat back on and went immediately to Camden's police station.

When Rose saw him, her eyes were bright with happiness. Her dear love was there to rescue her. A police sergeant directed him to a room and explained the situation. As James was a well-known gentleman, the police agreed to let her go with him under his supervision. He spoke to Sergeant Smith, who was in charge of the case, and told him all he knew about Rose and that he was eager to know about her too because he was to marry her. He advised the sergeant to keep it as a confidential matter.

When James and Rose were on their way to the house, he said, 'I do not quite understand who informed the police as not many people know about you. Have you got an idea who it could have been, Rose?'

'Darling, my only guess is Louise as she was very upset and jealous last time we saw her. Apart from her, I would have no idea.'

James said to her, very concerned, 'So we have to treat her with care to prevent complications. Darling, it would be good if you could remember what happens when you disappear.'

'I will do my best, darling. I love you.' She kissed him tenderly and continued, 'Darling James, have you noticed any change in my behaviour before I disappear?'

'Well, darling, you normally have disquieted moments before you vanish. I was surprised you did not disappear when you were at the police station.'

'Yes, darling, that was odd. I need to remember!' she said desperately.

James went to Rose, embraced her, and said, 'Darling, I should keep a diary of your disappearances so we can get back to it, and probably that can help you to remember.'

'I am scared, darling,' said Rose.

'I am too. I do not want to lose you. I would rather die,' James said, terrified.

'Please do not say that, darling. We have to be positive, and everything will be fine,' she said hopefully.

Amber was on the train, going to work, and when she realised, she discovered that she had missed her station. She immediately got off at the next stop and crossed to the other platform to get back. She managed to get to where she worked as a clerk just in time. Another day at work—her duties were just the same every day, but she enjoyed her work. Her colleagues were always greeting one another with a smile as if that was a rule to accomplish and no more. Most people did not answer their greetings as they were drowning in their work. Amber thought, *We can feel alone in a crowded home.*

It was 5.30 p.m.—time to go home! Amber tidied up her desk and went. Clapham Junction underground station was so crowded, and in the train, she felt squeezed like a sardine in a tin. When it was rush hour, she had to squeeze in or get home late. She got home, had something to eat, and prepared herself to connect to the Internet.

Although South America was very far, Amber still was in contact with her family, so she was up to date with her family's news. She always had to speak to her mother as she was much attached to her, and more than a mother, she was a friend. Hearing the voices of each of her dearest ones was a feeling that could not be replaced. One summer day, a Thursday, when Amber was at work, she received an email from her family. Her father had an operation. He was in his seventies but was still enthusiastic and active. Helping the community was his main goal before and after he retired. He suffered from diabetes, and his leg needed to be amputated. Amber phoned the hospital to speak to her father. 'Hello, Papa. How are you feeling?' she asked him worriedly. He was happy and said to her, 'Better than ever.'

'I am so pleased to hear your voice, Papa. We all love you, Father.' Amber was sobbing and told him that she was to fly to South America to see him. She kept on having a strange feeling as if something was not told. Mr Grajales, her papa, said to her that he was worried about her mother. Amber said to him, 'Mum will be fine. We will look after her, and I will be looking after the family unit. It will be my priority, I promise you.' Amber was crying, feeling that she was going to lose her father. Her boss at work, an English lady called Pamela, kindly helped Amber to book her flight and sent her home to pack her suitcase; her trip was booked for the coming Sunday. Amber also had a part-time job as a cashier in a well-known supermarket in London. Despite her feeling so emotional, she was compelled to do her shift that Saturday just before her trip, as if without her the company could not function.

Her line manager, an arrogant tall male, ignored her pain and suffering. The customers in the store were concerned, and they kept on asking Amber what the matter was. She could not speak as her pain was too great. At that moment in South America, her father died in a clinic. The operation was successful, but as there was blood streaming from the wound of his leg, a nurse decided to give an injection to him to stop the bleeding without realising it was going to induce his death. He had a respiratory attack and died instantly. A few minutes later, around 4 p.m., Joel came to the supermarket to give her the sad news. Amber broke down, sobbing loudly, wishing to have seen her father before he died. She left the till and took her belongings from her locker, accompanied by Joel. She told the South African manager that her family was her first priority and that he could keep the job. They left the store, and her mind was wondering about her manager's lack of humanity.

Amber was inconsolable the whole journey to South America. She was determined that she was to comfort her family, especially her mother. Her brothers were waiting at the airport for her, and she missed her parents as they used to be there every time she arrived from abroad. She got home at midnight. The house was crowded. All the neighbours and friends were looking at her, expecting a reaction when seeing her father's coffin, but Amber arrived home and calmly greeted some of them and looked for her family. Her mother and siblings were having sour orange-leaf tea to keep calm. Mrs Grajales was not showing her grief, but her pain was too great. The love of her life was gone. When the family was left alone in the house around 6 a.m., Amber asked Laura, her niece who was a very strong young woman and very closed to her, to open the coffin, which was placed in the sitting room. There were neither candles nor flowers around the coffin as opposed to the town's custom. This called the mourners' attention, but it was her father's will taken into account. He believed in God but did not agree with wake rituals. Amber went and looked at her father closely. Soon she realised that her mother was near her, looking at him too. Amber caressed her father's hand, which was very still, and she realised his hand was similar to hers. She thought, *Every time I look at my own hands, I will remember my father.* She felt happy to remember that she had the chance to say goodbye to her father last time they spoke on the phone. That was the greatest present he left her aside from the great relationship they had.

Rose was in the park again, and James was there waiting for her. The cold wind was embracing them, but this time, Amber could not feel it. 'Darling Rose,' he said, running towards her and embracing her, 'I was so anxious. You had not come for several days. The police were asking for you, and I was giving all sorts of excuses.'

'Oh, darling, I hope it is nothing serious. I am so glad to see you here. Let's go home,' Rose said, looking fatigued.

'Yes, darling, I missed you so much,' said James, pleased to see her.

They went home and went straight to her bedroom. Normally, she appeared late at night. 'Come, darling, have a rest. You look very tired. Let me make you a cup of tea.' She assented and said, 'Thank you, darling.'

Suddenly Rose felt terribly emotional. James came into the bedroom with the tea and saw her tearful. 'Darling, what is the matter?' he asked, concerned.

'I have just remembered my father,' she sobbed.

James became aware of the fact that Amber was recalling more things about her other life, and that was very important, so he kept her talking about it. 'What happened to your father, darling?' he asked eagerly.

'He died.' So she sobbed even more.

He embraced her and said, 'My sincere condolences, darling.'

Then Rose realised that she had remembered it. 'I am talking to you about my father,' she said.

'Yes, darling, please continue talking about your father,' asked James impatiently.

'I saw my father lying in a coffin, and my niece opened it so I could see him closer. Oh, darling, I actually need to go now as the funeral is taking place.' She sounded extremely stressed out. She knew she should take advantage of her stressed mood to disappear.

'Certainly, my darling, I will be waiting for you,' said James. He kissed her, and when he looked at the door and turned back, she was gone.

Amber appeared for the funeral. Her sister Bella, who had nursed her father during his illness, was crying incessantly, and the

townspeople thought she was the one who came from abroad. Amber
was calm. She did exactly what her father wanted her to do. She acted
calmly, remembering his words that we all were to die one day and
all that were left were the good remembrances. That was what gave
Amber comfort. *I treasure my father's memories*, she thought. The
funeral procession took place, and the coffin was taken straight to the
cemetery to the surprise of some of the mourners who were waiting for
them in the town's church.

After the funeral, Amber stayed with her family. Her sister Bella
disposed of her father's possessions a week after, just as she did when
her husband died. She thought it would help their mother to accept
her loss, but Amber felt it was too soon. Perhaps her mother would
have wanted to wait, but she was a quiet woman and did not say
much.

Now James was waiting for Rose in the park as usual. He ran to
her and embraced her. 'My darling Rose, I am so happy to see you.
How do you feel now?' asked James.

'I feel better, darling, thanks,' replied Rose.

'Let's go home,' James said tenderly.

When they were having supper, James told her that his mother
had invited herself to spend a few days with them. 'Please, darling, do
not be troubled,' he said to Rose. 'I have advised her to be kind to you,
otherwise she would not make me happy, and she has promised it.'

Mrs Gobbling came to visit James as arranged. Rose was ready for
the visit and was pleased to meet Mrs Gobbling, but she was distant
and almost treated Rose with contempt. Mrs Gobbling asked, 'Rose,
when are you planning to leave? Or are you staying longer?'

Rose did not know what to answer, and James came to her rescue.
'Please, Mother, I would appreciate if you remember your promise,' he
said patiently.

'But, James, son, do you not remember who the Gobbling family
is? What are we to tell our society?' she asked, concerned.

'Mother, you can say that Rose and I are engaged and that we will
confirm the wedding date in due course,' James said in earnest.

'James, son, you do not understand. Our society is going to ask
who she is, where she is from, so what am I to say?' she asked, terribly
upset about the situation.

'A solution will be found, Mother. Do not be preoccupied, please,' James answered, trying to calm his mother down.

Rose was feeling the pressure, and Mrs Gobbling's attitude towards her was not very positive.

The following morning, Mrs Gobbling went to Rose's room, but she was not there. She ran to James's room and knocked on his door. James got up and asked her, 'What is the matter, Mother?'

She replied, 'Son, I am afraid I have to tell you something very serious. Rose does not seem to have slept in her room.'

'Mother, please enjoy your stay and do not be worried about Rose. She is fine and will turn up any time,' James said in a relaxed way.

'What type of relationship is this?' asked his mother. 'Is it true that she is a flapper? Does she work in a club of some kind? Are you engaged to her? I should speak to your father immediately!'

'With all my respect, Mother, please remember that I am an adult and I have my private affairs to deal with. One day the situation with Rose will be clarified, but at the moment, I cannot do it. Please understand, Mother,' said James.

'Son, you are aware of who we are and what society we belong to, also our duties. As long as you honour the family name, your father and I will be at ease.'

Not long after her father's funeral, Amber went back to London. She was in her maisonette. She and Joel went to see the doctor as per a telephone call from the surgery that morning. The doctor told them that Joel was likely to get diabetes and that he needed to follow a especial diet. Joel was feeling down. Amber's father had diabetes, and deep inside, she was not feeling very strong. Even though she said to Joel, 'Darling, we already had the diet in action,' Joel read an information leaflet and said disappointedly, 'It is a forever illness.' The doctor tried to make him understand that if he lost some weight and kept the diet strictly, he might not need to prescribe him the tablets. Joel was as scared as Amber, but they both tried to be positive. Joel wanted to keep it a secret. Although Amber wanted to ask for help, she decided to keep it a secret and read some information about the illness on the Internet. She was feeling scared as she loved Joel very much. 'I do not want to lose you, darling,' she said desperately, sobbing.

Once again, Rose was in the park. James was not around, and she panicked. Then she thought, *I'd better go to James's home.* She remembered where the keys were hidden and opened the door. James was not in. She kept on waiting. The night came, but no news about James. She was unable to sleep. The next morning, someone knocked on the door. It was James's sister, Loren.

'Good morning, Rose. How are you?' said Loren courteously.

'Fine, thanks, Loren. Please come in,' said Rose.

Loren looked worried and said, 'Rose, I brought you some news about James.'

'What news?' she asked, concerned.

Loren said, 'James is staying at Mama's house.'

'Why?' Rose asked anxiously.

'Rose, please do not be worried. He has been terribly ill, but he is recovering now. It was a mild heart attack, but the doctor assured us he would be fine. James was very preoccupied about you, so he requested me to come and let you know about him.'

Rose sobbed and begged Loren, 'Can you take me to him, please?'

Loren said, 'Yes, of course, Rose. James will be very happy to see you.' So they went.

When Rose saw James on the bed, she ran to him and forgot the other people who were around. 'Darling, my darling, I did not know what happened to you. How are you feeling, my love?' she said with tears in her eyes.

He said to her, 'My darling Rose, I am fine. The doctor has advised that I should have some rest, but nothing major.'

'Could I look after you tonight?' begged Rose.

'That will be fine, Rose. You can stay with me.' She kept on embracing him as the thought of losing him in her absence made her cry even more. She wanted to tell him about Joel as she had remembered more about her other life, but she decided to wait until James was at home, feeling better.

James's mother and Louise came into the room and demanded Rose to leave the room, but James looked at them with disapproval and asked for Rose to stay. He said, 'Should any of you feel uncomfortable with Rose's presence, please kindly leave the room.' Mrs Gobbling and Louise were struck by James's words and made a gesture of dislike.

Loren was happy with her brother's attitude as she was learning to love Rose. She went and kissed her brother. Mr Gobbling said to James, 'You are in the wrong, son, but we cannot discuss it now. It is best for you to get well first.'

'Yes, Father, we shall discuss it when appropriate. The doctor said that my health has ameliorated and that I can return to my house tomorrow. My stay in Surrey Manor has done me good, but I suppose we all have to get back to normality. Shall we?' he said respectfully.

Mrs Gobbling approached her son and whispered to him, 'Dear James, I cannot allow your friend to stay with you in the same room tonight. As far as we know, she is not engaged to you, and the society's rules apply in this household.'

'Mother,' said James, 'if that is the case, I am afraid I shall leave with Rose tonight and not tomorrow.'

His father interfered. 'Mama, James needs some rest. Allow him to have his way. It will be just for one night.'

Rose humbly said to Mrs Gobbling, 'Madam, I have no problem with waiting for James at his place. I'd rather go before causing you any more problems.'

Louise said rudely and sarcastically, 'That is much appreciated, Rose. Thank you.'

And James responded, looking sternly at Louise, 'Have you all heard what I have just said? If Rose goes, I go.'

His father said, calmly grabbing Louise and his wife by their arms, 'Son, I should ask these ladies to follow me so Rose and you can have some privacy.'

'Thanks, Father,' James said, relieved. They left the room.

'Darling, I do not want to be an obstacle between you and your family,' Rose said to James, embracing him.

'My dear Rose, my parents mean well, and they know my thoughts about aristocratic standards. Please do not be worried about them.' He kissed her tenderly and continued, saying, 'You are the most important person in my life. You are my happiness, and I shall defend it no matter what.'

Rose was offered the guest room next to James's, so they talked until late.

'As we are not in the privacy of our house, I will need to sleep away from you. They would not believe if we were to tell them that we do not have that type of intimacy they are thinking about,' Rose said to James.

'It does not matter, my darling Rose. We shall be home tomorrow.' She kissed him tenderly and arranged his bed's blankets and left the room, looking at James with a sweet smile. James blew her a kiss.

Rose entered the guest room, and surprisingly, someone was waiting for her in the darkness.

'Rose, would you please close the door,' requested Louise.

'What are you doing in here?' asked Rose, feeling trapped and vulnerable.

'Dear Rose, I know all about you.'

Rose looked at her in amazement as it was not true; only James knew about her.

'You are no one. This country has no records about you. You are an intruder, and your place will be in prison,' said Louise, infuriated.

Rose started crying, feeling intimidated; she hurriedly went into the bathroom that was en suite and closed the door behind her. Louise knocked on the door and told her that there was no need to hide as they needed to talk. Rose asked her, 'About what? You just want me out of James's life, don't you?' Rose opened the bathroom door to see Louise's facial expression.

Louise said, enraged, 'James is my husband-to-be, and I should not have you between us!'

'Louise, I feel for you as you want James to love you, but he told you he sees you as a sister. So why don't you accept the situation and leave us in peace?' said Rose in a sedate manner.

'How dare you say that to me—you, Miss No One,' said Louise furiously.

Rose answered, 'I am not going to continue with this conversation and would ask you kindly to leave the room.'

Louise took her leave but stopped at the door to say, 'You have no idea who I am, and I shall get what is mine. You shall have joy while it lasts.' She smiled wickedly and closed the door behind her.

Rose was distressed and wanted to run and tell James about it, but she was too upset and scared about the type of society she was dealing with. She decided to calm herself down and went to bed. She thought, *Tomorrow will be another day.*

In the morning, James felt better and decided to order some breakfast. Once the maid left his room, he took the tray and looked for Rose's room and entered it. He put the tray on the bedside table and went to Rose. James gave her a tender kiss, and Rose opened her eyes and smiled. 'Darling Rose, did you sleep well?'

'Yes, darling, I did. Thanks. What about you, darling? What are you doing walking around?' asked Rose.

James said amusingly, 'My darling, I have no want to be far from you, if I can help it. Furthermore, my mother and Louise's attitude towards you, I cannot trust.' She embraced him, and they kissed.

'Can we go home today, darling?' Rose asked pleadingly.

'Yes, my darling, we leave today,' said James.

'Thanks, darling,' said Rose, relieved.

One morning, Amber woke up and could hear Joel's snoring. She put her arm around him. She remembered James and thought, *I am confused. Who is James? Was he in my dream? I do not remember much, but it makes me feel relaxed to think about him.*

'Love you. How is my girl this morning? Where is my breakfast?' Joel said to Amber tenderly. She got up and asked him, 'What would you like for breakfast, darling?'

'Cheese on toast, please,' Joel said.

Amber went to the kitchen, and while preparing breakfast, she was trying to recall her dream. *I feel very happy for whatever reason, and I do not care if I do not understand why I feel so satisfied with my life*, she thought. She kept on thinking about James while the toast was getting burnt, and that made Joel upset as he was impatiently waiting for his breakfast. Amber felt guilty and very anxious.

Rose appeared in the park, and James was there waiting for her. She looked very emotional. 'Darling Rose, what is the matter? Please tell me.' Rose could not speak, and they embraced each other tightly.

'If you do not have the desire to talk about it, you do not have to,' said James, very concerned.

They got home, and she kept on being upset. Her sadness was drowning her. James got her tea and asked her to drink it. His tenderness was making her feel worse, not because she did not like it but because she now recollected more and she felt troubled.

'Darling James, I love you,' she said. He replied, holding her hand, 'I do love you too, my lovely Rose.' They embraced again. 'I . . .' She was going to talk but broke down completely. He took her hand and asked her to follow him to her bedroom. He helped her to lie on the bed. She said, 'Please do not leave me, James.'

'I shall stay with you. Just close your eyes and try to sleep, darling. Do it for me,' he said sweetly.

She calmed herself down and fell asleep. He was lying next to her, looking at her sleeping. When she woke up, they went to the kitchen and prepared something to eat. Rose was more relaxed and started to talk.

'Darling, I remembered about me and my other life.'

'Tell me about it,' said James.

'I am not sure yet how I got here, but I live in London. It is the year 2011! Everything is different . . . people wear different clothing. I live with my husband—his name is Joel, and he seems to love me. I work in an office, and today was a stressful day. My boss was checking on me and asking me to do so much that I thought I should not be there. Then I got home, as always happy to see Joel, but his temper was just uncontrollable. A game of poker on the Internet stressed him out so badly, and he shouted at me for no reason and made me feel terrible. He demanded for me to leave him alone. I could not handle an evening of stress, and I said to him, "I will go as you wish." I went to the bedroom, and now I am here with you and I feel so happy. I know you might be disappointed because I am married, but that is the truth,' said Rose, relieved. 'I do not understand as we are here in the year 1960.' She was puzzled.

James did not know what to say; he was feeling confused too and rather disappointed but happy for her as she was finding things out about herself. 'Tell me, Rose, where do you live? Did your husband ask you about your absences? Are you happy?'

'Darling, please,' said Rose imploringly. 'I still do not know much about my situation. I have just remembered a few facts, but they can be past or present. I am afraid I do not have answers for all your questions yet.' Rose was feeling terribly confused.

Rose did not know how to approach James as she knew she was married and she could not call him *darling*. James was feeling the same uncertainty; he could not call her his darling as she belonged to another man.

'Rose, it is late, and if you are not to go yet, you need to rest,' James said, wanting to kiss her, but something did not let him do it.

Rose took his hand and said, 'Do not leave me now. I am scared, darling.' Rose's action made him feel alive again. It was needed. They went to her bedroom, and James fell asleep embracing her.

In the morning, he woke up, and she was there with his breakfast. She put the tray on the bedside table. 'I want to thank you, darling,' Rose said calmly.

'Whatever for?' he asked.

'Because you are so patient with me and my situation. Promise me that we will always be together,' she said with tears in her eyes. He got up and cuddled her. 'Of course, Rose, we will be always together, but . . .' James stopped.

'But what, darling?' she asked imploringly.

'Rose, you know you have a husband, and we should look for him. He might be looking for you.'

'Darling, my husband is not looking for me, I know.'

'Rose, does he have knowledge of your whereabouts?' He was confused.

'James, my darling, that is what I need to find out next time I disappear. Because I know my husband is not looking for me, perhaps he does not care about me.'

'Dear Rose, I am sure he loves you as I do. He is first, and I do not want to disrespect him or you. It is a very difficult situation,' James said, bewildered.

She cuddled him. 'I am very scared, darling. I need you!' said Rose, feeling lost.

He thought of his family and the possibility of them knowing about Rose's situation. Then he thought not to pay attention to what everyone else might think. He loved Rose, and he would stand by her. He had to make the most of the moments they could spend together, which perhaps might be their last moments, as she might not stay with him. James had various questions in his mind. Who was her husband?

Where was he living? Did she have children? Was she happy? Or probably she was unhappy, and that could be the reason why she did not want to remember. James needed to be strong and help Rose to untangle her life no matter what was in store for their relationship. He decided to write once again to Mr Darlington, the investigator. Mary, the maid recently recruited in James's house, happened to have heard their conversation. When she went to the post office to mail Jame's letter to Mr Darlington, she had a friendly conversation with the owner of the shop. 'Good morning, Mrs Griffin. Could you please send this letter as urgent?' Mrs Griffin was known to interfere in other people's private lives. She looked at the address and asked the maid for the reason it was to be urgent. The maid gave her the information she was after. 'The lady who came to stay with Mr Gobbling Junior was in trouble.'

'What kind of trouble?' the inquisitive woman asked.

'Well, I overheard that she has a husband.'

Mrs Griffin, showing her surprise and disapproval, said, 'She is an adulterer, and this situation is appalling.'

'Madam, please do not say it to anybody. I do not want to get into trouble,' pleaded the maid.

'Do not be preoccupied, my dear. They should know, what is done in the darkness will come to light sooner or later. Leave it to me. Go now,' she demanded.

The maid was feeling guilty for having told Mrs Griffin about Rose's situation, but she could not do anything to stop the gossip. Mrs Griffin wrote to Mr Gobbling Senior, requesting him to do something about the situation; otherwise, she was to tell the newspaper about it. Mr Gobbling wrote to his son, requesting an urgent meeting with him. Mrs Gobbling was terribly anxious. The letter was quite formal, and James was requested to visit the family by himself.

'Dear Rose, my father has written to me, requesting my presence, and I do not want to leave you alone. I have already asked the investigator to keep me informed of any new developments. We will soon have news, dear.' James was feeling apprehensive on how to treat Rose without hurting her. 'Rose, as my father did not mention the reason for requesting my presence at Surrey Manor, I hope Mother is not feeling unwell. I shall not be long.'

'That's fine, James,' she said with sadness. She could also feel the distance between them. 'James, dear,' she called him before he went.

'Yes, Rose, what is it?'

'I want to say that I do understand the situation, and I am not going to misunderstand your changes in treating me. I know that the fact of being married to someone else is very serious. I do hope we can find out more information soon.' She gave him a cuddle, and he corresponded. He did not want to lose her; that was the last thing James wanted to happen. Rose was the love of his life, and Rose felt the same towards him. When he arrived home, his father was waiting for him in the study.

'How is my son?' said Mr Gobbling proudly, and they both were happy to see each other. They talked about the weather and possible pheasant hunting. Then Mr Gobbling started to mention his ancestors and the society's conventions to end up talking about Rose. 'Son, do you know who this woman is? Is there any history attached to her? What is her family name? And so on and so forth.'

'Father, my life has changed since I met Rose. She is my especial friend, and I have no access to her personal details due to circumstances I could not explain at the moment. All I know is that Rose is such a wonderful woman with some natural qualities. What society might say about us does not concern me.' Mr Gobbling asked him to be more aware of the surroundings, and James said, 'I cannot waste my time thinking of society's trivialities and conventions, Father. You know the way I have thought since I was very young, and that has not changed. Rose has not done anything incorrect. We are friends, and for reasons that I cannot explain, she is living in my house. She is a respectable woman, and I will protect her from whoever wants to hurt her.' Mr Gobbling decided to stop the conversation as he agreed with James; he knew James and respected his views. He decided to leave the matter to him. James was determined to stand up for himself and for what he believed.

Mrs Gobbling, on the other hand, had promised Louise to help her get rid of Rose to conform with the society's rules. 'Dear Louise, please understand James. He is just helping this poor woman who is mad but pretty. Any man would have taken the opportunity.'

'No, madam,' said Louise. 'He is in love with her, and now he will not marry me.' She cried loudly. 'What am I to do?' Louise said desperately.

'Do not be troubled, girl. We will do something about it,' Mrs Gobbling said confidently.

Amber was seated on the sofa. Joel had not gone back from work yet. She found an old-fashioned key in her pocket, and she wondered why this key was not with the other ones in her camel key ring. When Joel got home, she asked him about the key, and Joel said he did not know. He had not seen the key before. He was interested in antiques, so he advised Amber to keep it as it could be of value.

Amber was feeling bewildered as she had the urge to discover the mystery, and she did not quite understand what it was. Joel came to keep her company and said, 'Darling, are you feeling unwell? You look a bit anxious. Is everything all right?'

'Yes, dear,' she said, unsure.

Early winter morning, Amber went to her new job. She was, as usual, enjoying reading a book on the train on her way to work. Her boss was an Irish lady, but to Amber, she was the first Irish person who was so cold towards her. She was dominant and racist towards the non-European foreigners. Amber was trying to get on with her. Her boss was good at manipulating people and on making people believe she was always right. Amber, being a soft character, always apologising for what she had not done, made her vulnerable, so she was now a target for the bullies. Her father and mother used to protect her when she was young. Then Joel was her protector, but at work, she felt unprotected.

Amber woke up one morning, and all she could think about was the name James. She could not understand the reason she was thinking about him, but she was sure he existed in her life. 'I need to know what is going on with me. I seem to have a lover, and his name is James. But I am not sure how I can contact him,' Amber said to herself.

Amber started looking through her belongings and could not find a sign of James. *I seem to love him. I need to find something about him, or I am going to think that I am going mad*, she thought. She emptied her handbag and checked her little purse. She saw again the old door key. She thought, *This is not our door key. It has to be James's. I know it is real, and I feel I'm in love with James, but where is he?* Amber was feeling nervous as she knew she was faithful to Joel and she could not be facing an adulterous relationship. She was so worried as she could not find an explanation to what was happening. When she was lying in bed with Joel, she kept on looking at him, feeling guilty, and that was incomprehensible.

Most of the nights, Joel woke up and asked her why she could not sleep, and she always answered that she had insomnia and she would try to sleep.

One sunny morning, Amber was feeling so anxious that she forgot to pack her lunch. She could not accept that she could be unfaithful to Joel. She tried to focus on her work to have no time to think and feel so much guilt.

Once again, Rose appeared in the park; James was there, happy to see her. 'James, my love, I missed you! Take me with you.' He took her by the hand, and they went home.

'Do you want to make love to me, darling James?'

James replied, 'You are married, my darling, and it is better to keep our relationship as it is. My comfort is to see you and have the hope that one day you can be my wife.'

Amber assented and said, 'You are right, darling. We should be patient and continue searching for answers. I also hope we can get married in the future.'

James said, 'I will always be your especial friend, and I am sure one day you will be free to go to the altar with me—that is my dream.' She embraced him as she felt loved and protected by him.

Miriam and Amber were walking along Wimbledon Common. Miriam said, 'It is so lovely to feel the peace and freshness of the common.'

'I feel the same. It is a spiritual peace where you have no grudges towards anybody. You love everyone even more, especially your family and friends,' said Amber.

'Is this the kind of peace that people feel when they are dead?' Miriam asked Amber.

'If that is, I am ready to die any time,' Amber said placidly.

'What about Joel, Amber?' Miriam asked.

'He is fine, thanks. I hardly see him as he works nights,' Amber replied.

Miriam told her that her relationship with her husband was getting better and they wanted to keep the family together. She was happy for their son as he was the one who missed him the most. Miriam's feelings were not the same. She was less emotional and more factual.

Rose appeared in the park once again. James was happy to see her. They hugged each other. 'My dear Rose, where have you been? I have been waiting for days and not a sign of you,' he asked, concerned.

'Darling, I am so glad to have come back,' said Rose happily. The park was also looking in a stately splendour as spring was announcing its entrance.

They made their way to James's house. Once they were in, she sweetly hugged him and kissed him tenderly, and he could not help but correspond to her. 'I missed you so much,' she said, and he answered, 'I missed you even more, my darling. How have you been? I was immensely worried about you.'

'Now I know what is going on,' said Rose.

'Tell me, darling,' he asked enthusiastically.

'I think I am living a double life, darling,' said Rose.

'What? What sort of double life?' James asked, surprised.

'Darling, I can now remember what my present is,' she said.

'This is your present, dear Rose,' he replied.

'Darling, I am in a dream. You are my dream, but it is so special because it does not happen or it is not normal to be able to close your eyes so many times and keep on being in the same dream, but I can do it. I do not know yet what triggers it. What is so important for me is that I can come back to you, my darling,' said Rose.

'I am happy for that, Rose, although I do not understand how I can be in a dream. You are not in a dream—you are here. I can touch you and kiss you,' James said, feeling confused.

'I know, darling. That is why I said this is not a common dream. It is something out of the ordinary, and I feel very happy about it. I love you, darling. Can you love two people at the same time? I am trying not to get confused or preoccupied about this situation. I just want to enjoy it while it lasts,' said Rose.

James was disturbed; he did not know what to say. 'Darling, tell me, what is your other life?' he asked impatiently.

'I know my name is Amber, and I do not have children. I live in Wimbledon, but I am from South America. I work as a clerk. I am not happy in my relationship with my husband as his temper is unbearable due to his gambling addiction. Although I see some other people around, I am not sure yet who they are. Darling, please allow me to live this fantastic moment with you. I feel somehow free of guilt as I know I am not unfaithful to my husband. The idea of being unfaithful is not for me. I have my family principles. This case is quite rare, and I have decided to live my dream with you. I am not hurting Joel, and I hope I am not hurting you.'

She smiled at him and held his hand. 'Darling, we are always to be together. Nothing and no one can come between us and our love,' she said positively.

James was feeling unsure about the situation but decided to follow Rose's words and enjoy the moment of love they were living. He approached her tenderly and cuddled her. 'I love you, darling, and I have no wish to lose you, so I am in agreement. Let's enjoy the time together no matter what. So now that we know your real name, shall I call you Amber instead of Rose?' asked James.

Rose replied, 'No, my darling, I love the name you gave me. I will always be your Rose.'

Amber woke up, and Joel was there. It was time to go to work, so Amber got up happily and got dressed. She put on some perfume and kissed Joel.

Joel was very unsure; he sometimes wondered why Amber was suddenly in such a happy mood, but he did not talk about it. He smiled and thought about how beautiful Amber looked and how much he loved her. One day at work, Amber and Jessie were in the massage room, one of the meeting rooms in the company. It was almost a ritual for them to meet there at lunchtime and talk about their lives or advise each other or share a joke. Although they were from different backgrounds, their ways of thinking were quite similar. Jessie was from the Caribbean. She was a well-spoken young woman with a strong character. She was tall and heavyset, very confident and fearless, and quite popular in the office. Jessie advised Amber to be more assertive and less sensitive; otherwise, she could not survive the office environment. She was a softie, and that meant weakness, therefore prone to be bullied.

Jessie taught Amber about the office life. She advised her convincingly, 'Three things you need to remember: Do not take anything to heart. You do not come to make friends. Do your job and go home. That's all.'

'I will, Jessie,' said Amber. Jessie offered Amber a sort of protection, and in a way, Amber felt secure.

Jessie was married, and she was the boss in her house. She loved her husband, Jim, also from the Caribbean; according to her, it was a match made in heaven. One day while in the massage room, Jessie opened her heart and told Amber that she wanted to go back home to spend some time with her mother as she missed her terribly. Jim, her husband, was stopping her from doing it as he liked going to Jamaica for a short holiday. Amber said to Jessie that it was a very difficult situation and it was up to Jessie to make her decision, and Jessie agreed. Amber's dream was so personal that not even Jessie or her friend Miriam could know about it. She wanted to keep it to herself.

'James, darling!' Rose said.

James ran to her and embraced her. 'Where have you been, my darling? I was worried sick. It was so frustrating not to be able to contact you,' said James, concerned.

'Darling, do not get tired of my situation. I will find a way to communicate with you from wherever I am. Now I know that when I think of you and wish to come to you, I can do it! It's wonderful! Don't you think?' she said happily.

'Yes, my darling, but my dream is not to have you far from me. I shall wait patiently, I promise,' he said sweetly.

'How can I not love you, James? You are the most patient and tender person I have ever known.'

James smiled and sweetly caressed her hair and said, 'Darling, the feeling is mutual. I could not live without your smile and loving heart.' They decided to go home.

When in the house, James said to Rose tenderly, 'Darling, shall we have some tea? It is so delightful to have you by my side.' He looked at her with love.

'Oh, my love, I am extremely happy to be with you.' She gave him a kiss on his lips and went to make the tea hurriedly. While in the kitchen, she saw an envelope on the kitchen board. She read it and knew it was from James's father.

She brought the tea and told him he had forgotten a letter in the kitchen. He did not want to talk about it, so he only said, 'I will pick it up before going to bed.' As Rose was so respectful of James, she decided to wait for James to tell her about the letter.

He approached her and kissed her tenderly on her lips and told her how much he was missing her. 'Have you got any more news, darling?' James asked.

Rose responded, 'Well, not really, darling. I know how to come back and see you, and I still do not know how I move from one time and place to another. This is extraordinary—only you know about it. I have not told my friend Miriam about us as she loves talking to people and she may have a slip of the tongue about my secret.'

'It is my want to make sure we will always be in communication, and you shall come to see me as I cannot control time and visit you, my darling,' said James.

'I promise you this is a forever relationship, and no one should take us apart ever. Please promise me, darling, that you will wait for me no matter what. I belong to you, and you belong to me,' said Rose, expecting an immediate response from James, but he hesitated as if something did not allow him to be too certain about it. 'Rose, I will always love you, and you know that. I will be always here for you, and I trust you will come here and look for me.'

Rose looked at him and hugged him, and he responded hurriedly and passionately to that hug. They tenderly kissed as if they were engaged for life. Rose disappeared again, but this time for a much longer period.

Rose appeared in the park once again. She did not find James waiting for her, so she decided to go to James's house. Her key was not of use as the lock was changed. She knocked on the door, expecting the maid to appear, but instead, Louise opened the door. She looked at Rose with surprise and said rudely, 'Yes, Rose, how can I help?'

Rose was completely speechless. She answered Louise angrily, 'I need to see James. Where is he?'

'Oh, you are referring to my husband, is that correct?' said Louise proudly.

Rose could not believe what she heard. 'Listen, Louise, I just want to know about James. Where is he?' Rose tried to calm down.

'You have no right to know about James's whereabouts, but as I am the lady of this house and I should be polite, I shall tell you that James is on a business trip. We got married a year ago. He loves me, and he told me that there was no relationship between you and him and that you were just a good friend, that was all,' Louise said spitefully.

Rose was still in shock; she did not understand what was going on. She left and walked towards the park. It was full of memories. She sat on the usual bench, feeling alone and with tears on her cheeks. She thought, *Why did I come back? Why did I stay too long in my other world? Is it only to regret and feel anger to have seen Louise as the lady of the house? How humiliating!* She could not stop crying and thinking where she was supposed to go as James was not waiting for her.

Suddenly a familiar voice took her out of her pensive mode. Loren, James's sister, appeared and approached her. 'Dear Rose, long time since I last saw you. Oh, you are crying!' She embraced her.

'I have just been told about James's marriage to Louise, and I am broken-hearted.'

'Dear Rose, James loves you dearly, but as it took you so long to return and the family was in a state of difficulty that needed to be resolved, he was compelled to marry Louise. He is not a happy man, I assure you,' said Loren.

'I know,' Rose responded. She felt so much guilt about it. It was all her fault, she thought. She could not forget him—that was completely impossible. Her suffering was intolerable. There was nothing she could do to change the situation. Louise was his wife, and that was not going to change. Perhaps it was to happen like this because she could not be allowed to love two people at the same time. That would be unfair. She could not contain her tears; she knew James was not to be blamed. There was nothing she could do to help him to not feel as miserable as she was.

'Dear Rose, I know Mama will be happy to have you. Come with me. You do not have a place to go to,' said Loren.

'Your mother does not like me, Loren. My presence will make her feel uncomfortable,' said Rose.

'Please do not be preoccupied, Rose. Mama has changed and has realised that Louise is not the one for James. She suffers for him and his unhappiness.'

Rose agreed to go with Loren as she needed a place to stay.

'I am exceedingly concerned about James. I know he loves you, and he knows you will be back,' said Loren.

James could not stop thinking about Rose and could not help being anxious about what could be happening to her. He was wishing he could change his life. His only comfort was his child. The circumstances had pushed him to marry Louise. He definitely knew he could never love another woman besides Rose, and Louise knew it but kept the hope that James would love her eventually. Louise did not tell James about Rose's visit; she decided to keep it to herself. She did not want to jeopardise what she called their happiness.

Loren explained the situation to her mother, and she decided to put her up for the time being. She had to speak to Mr Gobbling. He would be happy to see her as he knew his son would be happy about the news.

'Dear Rose, please be our guest. I know you will have the chance to meet gentlemen who might be interested in you and marry you—someone who can replace my son,' said Mrs Gobbling. For Rose, hearing Mrs Gobbling say these words was like a knife pushed in her heart, unbearable to suffer in silence. Rose respected Mrs Gobbling and the family, so she did not say a word, but tears streamed down her cheeks. She quickly dried them before Mrs Gobbling could notice them.

As Rose was more in control of her disappearances, she decided to say to Loren that she would need to think about her life. She said sadly to Loren, 'Would you please keep in touch with James? I will go now for a long period, but I will come back. Please tell my darling James that no one will ever stop me from loving him the way I do. Distance and time will not stop me either.' Rose was devastated.

Loren took Rose to her bedroom and asked her to be patient and not to leave yet as she would try to help her to meet James.

Rose's eyes lit up as if that tiny hope was still there waiting to be taken. She said to Loren, 'Thanks very much for your words as they do give me comfort and some kind of hope.'

Rose sat down at a small desk and, looking through the window, saw the night entering the room. She could not see the stars or the moon but still felt the calm of the night. She thought, *I am also married, and I love my husband. Who am I to bother James's new life? He took the decision to marry Louise as she knew him before me. They both were single. Why am I to interfere in their lives? My darling husband is with me, so I am the only one living this confusing type of life, and I need to take the decision not to appear in this town ever again. James is gone, and there is nothing to keep me here. I came by accident and keep on coming by accident. This is a nice dream but just a dream.* Tears came down her cheeks.

Meanwhile, Louise and James were experiencing their lives together. Louise said to James, 'You know, I have always loved you, darling.'

James was silent as if he were in another world, hardly paying attention to Louise's words.

'Darling, did you hear what I said?' asked Louise impatiently.

James responded plainly, 'Yes, I heard you, dear.'

'Are you not going to say anything else?' Louise asked angrily.

'What am I supposed to say?' he said calmly, almost hopelessly.

'Nothing, I am starting to realise Mama was right. Obviously, I did not listen,' she said abruptly. She went to her room, crying. She was terribly in love with James, and what she thought was going to be her happiness turned out to be her nightmare. 'I have to make James forget Rose,' she determinedly said to herself, drying her tears.

Time passed by, and now Loren knew about Rose's secret life. Loren was a possible hope between James and her. Loren told Rose that she had seen James and that he did not look well. 'Why, what is going on with him? Please tell me,' Rose worriedly asked Loren.

'Well, he does not look as happy as before. Now he does not want to go to his factory, attend balls, or walk to the parks because he does not have any interest. He looked pale, and I asked him to see the doctor,' said Loren.

'Loren, I need to see him. I need to make sure he is fine,' Rose said, extremely worried.

'How and where can this meeting be arranged? I will invite him here. Louise does not know you are here, so it might be easier. Leave it to me, Rose. I will do my best as it has been months since he last came to see Mama. That is not like him. I am worried too,' said Loren with sadness.

Loren went to see James, but Louise did not allow them to be alone. 'Mama sent a message with me, James. She needs to speak to you. When can you come? I did not invite Louise as she is not on good terms with Mama,' said Loren.

'I know I am a bad son, husband, brother, and friend,' said James, feeling frustrated.

'Dear James, please do not say these things,' said Loren almost in tears. She embraced him and whispered in his ear, 'I shall help you get back to normal.' She said this, taking advantage of the time when Louise went to the kitchen. 'Can you come to see Mama tomorrow at 4 p.m.? Is that convenient?' Loren asked.

'Yes, I want to see Mama, and that will do me good,' said James.

Amber was in her bedroom, trying to analyse all that was happening to her. She was folding some clothes, and a paper came out of Joel's pocket. *It is happening again, oh God!* she said to herself. She took the paper and felt restrained to look at it as if it were a sin to see it without permission. She hesitated but decided to look at it. It was a receipt of money spent. He was gambling again. Amber's nightmare was not over. She thought, *How can he be so weak? He is chasing his losses. That is the typical symptom of a gambler.* Amber was disturbed and helpless.

Suddenly Amber's phone rang. It was Joel on the other line. 'Hello, darling,' he said amorously, 'how are you feeling?'

Amber answered warmly, 'Fine, darling.' It was the weekend, and she was determined to have a relaxed one. Also, Amber was feeling frustrated about James having got married with Louise, and she thought, *Was it love what we had, or was it a dream? A weird dream.* She could not help her tears, and she did not want Joel to see her like that. As the truth could not be told, Joel would not understand and would take it differently. He would think that James was real and that she was unfaithful to him.

She decided to have a shower so fresh Amber could come out of the bathroom. Joel was feeling playful and decided to enjoy the Friday evening together. He had promised not to gamble any more, just as he had done many times before. Amber had the hope that one day he would change his attitude towards gambling before it would be too late. She was feeling depressed and remembered the book she had read which was called *The Mayor of Casterbridge*.

Rose appeared in Surrey Manor, and Loren was the first one to see her as she was walking through one of the gardens. 'Dear Rose, I am so glad you have returned! How are you feeling? Would you tell me about what was happening in your other life?' Loren asked happily.

Rose replied, 'It is all complicated to explain, and I feel exhausted, Loren. Would you mind if I retired to my room?'

Loren softly said to Rose, 'I am sorry you feel that way, dear. Please go and have a rest.' But Rose was very anxious.

Amber got home from work. She was feeling exhausted as a new system had been introduced at work. There was high security in the company, specially for the last two on the pyramid, which were Amber and Jessie. Amber thought this was a way to guard them and keep them away from suspicion and fraud. Everyone was set up to get access to all the data, except the two of them. If anything were to happen, they would be the first ones to be investigated. What a joke!

Amber was definitely not happy at work. She could not communicate with some colleagues as they were looking down on her. Her boss was ill-treating her, and she felt trapped because she could not complain to anyone. It was her word against theirs, so she felt she had no chance. She made a cup of hot chocolate and went to the sitting room to unwind. She remembered her mother's sweet face and her father's smile, which usually used to give her peace and tranquillity.

Rose appeared in the park; she had the hope to see James. That little hope made her heart pump faster. As usual, she waited, and nothing happened. James was with his wife, who was giving him all the love that Rose could not give. A sad feeling took over her as she was longing to see him again. She was not going to give up on her dream.

Loren saw her across the street and called her over. 'Rose, I knew you would come,' she said happily.

'Hello, Loren,' Rose said pleasantly. She felt that part of James was there, still waiting for her. Loren asked her to go with her to her family house. 'You know, Rose, Mama loves you dearly and said you are like a daughter to her.'

'How kind of her,' said Rose gratefully.

'Let's go home,' said Loren enthusiastically. They both went happily.

The following morning, Rose decided to go and knock on Loren's bedroom door. She asked who was there, and Rose answered it was her, so Loren opened the door. Loren was not happy. Rose noticed she had been crying.

'What's wrong, Loren?' Rose asked anxiously.

'Nothing,' Loren said.

'Oh no, you are not crying just because of nothing. Tell me what is going on, please,' asked Rose, very concerned. Loren burst out in tears, and Rose embraced her and gave her comfort. 'Loren, please, what is the matter? I might be able to help you,' pleaded Rose.

Loren hesitated but decided to tell her. 'Rose, I am terribly in love with someone, but I see no hope. You cannot help me, no one can,' said Loren hopelessly.

'Who is he, Loren?' asked Rose.

'He is James's friend. His name is Paul, but Papa would not approve of him, and he does not even know how I feel about him. He only knows me as James's little sister! Oh, Rose, I do not know what to do.' Loren started crying. Rose embraced her and said, 'Listen to me, Loren. I am going to see Paul and tell him about your feelings towards him. We need to find out if he feels the same.'

'Would you do that for me?' Loren excitedly spoke.

Rose thought, *I would love for my situation to be as easy to solve as Loren's.* She could not have hope. James was married, therefore completely impossible for her.

'I know how much you suffer, Rose. I know how much you love James,' said Loren.

Rose assented and changed the topic about James. 'Loren, I am going to have a walk, and on my way, I will try to speak to Paul,' said Rose. Loren smiled, full of hope.

Rose went to Paul's office, and the clerk let Paul know that Rose wanted to see him. He immediately asked Rose to come inside his office.

'Rose, how delightful to see you. It has been a long time since I last saw you,' he said pleasantly and continued, 'Please be seated. How can I help?'

Rose went straight to the point. 'Oh, Paul, I am so pleased to see you too and glad you remembered me. I came here to talk to you about a young lady who is suffering, and I would love to put her out of her misery, if possible,' said Rose, determined.

Paul was eager to know more. 'May I know who is feeling miserable and why?'

'Her name is Loren Gobbling,' Rose said firmly.

When Paul heard her name, he was concerned as that name was very familiar to him. 'What happened to sweet Loren? James's little sister!' he asked.

'Yes, she is James's sister, and she is in love with you,' Rose said.

'Are you sure Loren has feelings for me?' he immediately asked.

'Yes, she confessed it to me, Paul. Now the question is, can you reciprocate her feelings?' asked Rose.

'Oh, dear Rose, what great news you have brought me. I've always loved Loren from a distance, but I had no courage to express my feelings to her,' he said and continued, 'When can I see her?'

Rose was so happy to know he was experiencing the same feeling for Loren and said to him, 'There is going to be a tea party at Surrey Manor this coming Saturday, and she has sent you an invitation.'

'I will be there, Rose. It will be splendid to see her. Please give my regards to all the family and especially to Loren. I am really delighted about the news and looking forward to see my sweet Loren,' said Paul happily.

'Paul, there is something I need to make you aware of. Loren told me that her father might have plans for her and that he might not find you as a suitable husband for his daughter.'

'Please have no worries, Rose. Mr Gobbling will willingly receive my offer, be reassured. I feel like the most fortunate man on earth!' he said.

The tea party took place, and Loren was waiting anxiously for Paul's arrival, she wished Amber had been there but she had disappeared again. Paul was announced to her parents. They were courteous with him. 'So, dear Paul, how is your business?' asked Mr

Gobbling. Paul had a newspaper business that had been passed on through the family from generation to generation.

'It is going very well, sir,' Paul replied enthusiastically.

'Are there any good stories on the pipeline?' asked Mr Gobbling.

'Yes, sir, we always have good stories to tell. By the way, sir, I would like to arrange an audience with you regarding an important matter, whenever convenient,' he asked Mr Gobbling.

Mr Gobbling sensed what was going to happen. Even though he knew that the young man was now in a very good position, he decided to give himself time, not showing too much eagerness. 'Dear Paul, would you come to Surrey Manor next Tuesday at 2 p.m., if convenient?' asked Mr Gobbling.

'Very well, sir,' Paul said eagerly before excusing himself as he was longing to meet Loren, who was looking at what was happening.

'That is fine,' said Mr Gobbling.

Rose appeared once again in the park. Unexpectedly, she saw a man seated on the bench where James used to sit waiting for her. She kept on approaching the bench as she could not recognise who he was. Then suddenly she realised that it was James! He looked at her, and his eyes were showing his affliction but with a light of happiness in them. They both felt unsure about what should be said.

'James, what are you doing here?' Rose asked sweetly. She could not believe it. She was dreaming about seeing him there, and it was happening. Her heart was beating rapidly.

'I was waiting for you, and I had a strong feeling today was to be the day. I am so pleased to see you, my darling Rose!'

'I am happy to see you too.' She wished to say *darling*, but she stopped herself from doing it. 'What is wrong, James? Where is Louise?' asked Rose worriedly.

'Louise and little James are home.' He felt sorry to say *home*. He wished to say 'our home, my darling', but he could not say it; that would hurt Rose, so he stopped himself short.

They stayed quiet for a few minutes, then Rose said, 'Oh darling, my darling, how can I bear my feelings towards you? I loved you since we met the first time, and it is still the same now.'

James looked at her with tenderness. 'It is exactly what is happening to me. That is the reason I am here. Loren told me about you, and I needed to see you, Rose. It makes me feel better. Why did destiny throw us apart when we love each other so dearly?' said James melancholically.

'I could not come back for a couple of years, and you could not wait for me. I do not blame you,' Rose said, feeling guilty.

'My darling Rose, the marriage with Louise was arranged as per family business, and I was so sad and weak without you, so I had no energy to go against it. But I have not stopped my love for you. I never lost the hope that we could be together again.' When Rose heard him, she could not resist embracing him and kissing him.

'My darling James, I love you so much. Forgive me, my darling, for not coming sooner to spare you the pain,' she said, mortified. They kissed with passion.

'My darling, I still have a house in the outskirts. Shall we make it our new meeting place? Please agree. I am dying for you,' said James imploringly.

'Let's go, darling, no time to waste,' said Rose with eagerness. They called a carriage and went. Once there, their passion came out, and their love was consumed. They forgot all the obstacles they had. James kept on kissing and caressing her as if it were the last time he was to see her.

'Promise me you will always come back, my darling,' said James.

'Yes, I promise, my darling. Nothing and no one can separate us ever,' said Rose.

'Could we stay here tonight, darling?' Rose asked.

James assented and said, 'Louise knows that I am on a business trip, so there is no problem at all, my darling.' They decided to live the moment, talking, playing with each other, promising not to be apart any more no matter what. They loved each other so intensely that there was no other feeling that could surpass their love.

'My darling, I missed you so much. It is here that I found the peace that I need to continue living,' said Rose happily.

'I know that, my darling,' said James, kissing her head and embracing her.

'Darling, there is so much going on with my life with Joel. I just wanted to get out of it. I am so glad you were waiting for me,' said Rose.

'My darling, you know that my marriage was not based on love but society's convenience. You are my spiritual wife forever and ever,' said James. Rose embraced him, and some tears ran through her cheeks.

'Why are you crying, my love?' asked James.

'Because I wish our love could be real,' she answered sadly.

'It is real, my love,' he said.

'Sorry, my darling, I am just desperate to stay with you, but my life's changes keep on happening. One day, just before I met you, when I was looking for Joel, I saw him gambling in a local betting shop. I burst out in tears, and at that moment, I felt someone's hands on my shoulders and heard a whispering voice telling me, "It is all right, my dear. Go home and keep holding on to those ancient presents." I felt strange but relieved. It sounded like the voice of an old man, and when I turned around, he was not there. Suddenly I remembered the feather Joel gave me in the past.'

James said, 'It is very interesting and mysterious! Do you still have this feather? Do you know what bird it comes from?'

'No, darling, all I know is that it is very ancient and I was supposed to look after it.' And she continued telling the story how Joel managed to get the three items in his possession.

'I am glad you told me this, Rose, because now I think that the feather might have something to do with what you are experiencing. I might be wrong, but it could be a possibility.' James gave her a strong hug and said convincingly, 'Darling, I always knew you were a very especial person, and that makes me feel more attached to you. I belong to you, and you belong to me, my darling—that is the way it is and will always be.'

They had a shower together. Every moment of intimacy was so precious for them. Rose felt so emotionally attached to James that she decided to take his hand, lead him to the bedroom, and make love once again. It was just the ultimate feeling before she disappeared once again.

Amber woke up and looked at her alarm clock on her bedside table. It was 3 a.m. Joel was asleep. She felt cold. It had been a long cold winter. The coldness of her relationship with Joel was making her feel unsure, as if there was no light at the end of the tunnel.

There was nothing that could motivate her to do anything. No more redecorations in the house, no flowers, just the feeling of a peaceful sad life ready to be buried.

Time was passing by. She had the same routine—going to work every morning and visiting Miriam every Friday. They had the same conversation about loneliness and not finding any motivation. Then she would go home to face Joel's moods and his problems. There was one thing that kept Amber going, and that was her family back in South America. She was always in touch with them through the Internet, where she met a young man to whom she felt attracted, so she booked her ticket to South America.

Months later, Rose appeared in the park again, and James was waiting for her. They looked deep into each other's eyes and hugged. They stayed silent for a few minutes. This was their way of talking, saying how much they missed and loved each other. He took her face and kissed her lips passionately.

'Say no words, my darling Rose. Just let me enjoy this moment with you and let me love you.' They entwined in a passionate kiss, forgetting all about the recriminatory glances and comments of passers-by.

Rose said, 'Darling, let's go to our nest, where we can be ourselves and live our precious moments together.' Rose could not help feeling very emotional and extremely happy being with James.

James knew her so well. After having some tea and settling down, James embraced her sweetly and invited her to sit in front of the fireplace.

'I want you to remember, my sweet James, that I will never stop loving you. You are my life, and without you, I have no life,' she said gratefully. They kissed passionately.

'Would you like to talk about what happened with Joel, my darling? Only if you want to talk about it,' said James kindly.

'Darling James, I thought I fell in love with someone else in the other world. I thought about it, but it was not real love. I had a hope that someone could love me and care for me. I was wishing for a love like ours, but in reality. Unfortunately, it does not exist! No one can love me the way I can love,' said Rose. James embraced her and said, 'Perhaps you have to come to terms and accept my unreal real love, as I can love you the way you love me, my Rose.'

'Darling, how can I be in this turmoil of feelings? My life on the other side is just a complete chaos, and I just want to be with you in peace, us loving each other, feeling the real love in this world where we are, my darling. I want to stay forever here. I do not want to go back to the other side, my darling,' said Rose in agony.

'We shall find a way to be together forever and ever. Tell me, darling, what has been happening,' asked James anxiously.

'Too many things, my darling,' she said desperately. Rose's memories flashed back, and she told James all that was going on. Amber had left Joel as her feelings for him were not the same. She wanted to live her life and was waiting for a change, even desiring to find someone who could love her.

One day Amber was online. She was looking at her niece Vicky's profile where she found some weird messages from someone called David. His profile picture was of a tall man, well built, with a long ponytail. He looked quite attractive, and he seemed to like heavy metal music, gothic girls, and darkness. Also he appeared on his profile as a professional with a University degree. David lived in the same town as Vicky; that made Amber very concerned as she had heard news on TV about people appearing online and giving false information just to play with silly girls. Amber wanted to find out more about David just to make sure no harm would come to her niece. He kept writing on Vicky's profile about his dark world. Vicky was a girl with all the attributes of an attractive young brunette. She was eighteen years old, very sensitive, naive, and religious. Vicky told Amber that she felt very scared of David's pictures shared online. According to his profile, he was unknown to the town; all they knew about David was his date of birth and his age as he appeared to be thirty years old. It seemed he wanted to catch Vicky's attention through messages about Satan and his disbelief in the Christian faith; on the other hand, he seemed to have developed feelings for Vicky as love messages started to appear. As Amber was much attached to her family and would always try to help them, she took a decision and started to communicate with David, trying to call his attention and know more about him. Amber was online more often, adding comments to his messages to Vicky, and he got interested in Amber's messages. David started focusing his attention on Amber, trying to find out more about her. She felt so attracted for what he was writing to her, so they started writing to each other. The time passed, and every day at the same time, Amber was there for him to chat online. Amber stopped disappearing. She wanted to see James, but she could not. Amber felt that she had let James and Joel down by getting distracted by David's infatuation. Amber and David were separated by a glass wall.

They made so many plans and even thought of having a baby, getting married—so many things. When Amber went to see him, she discovered that David's picture on his profile was not him, and he looked very slim and much younger than expected. The description of being a professional was not true. The only description that was right was that he was younger than her. She faced lies, but Amber decided not to stop there as the attraction for him was greater. They started getting to know each other, sharing great moments together. Amber began to know the real David. He was a fanatic of the heavy metal movement, and that thought made Amber uneasy. She felt the need to help him get out of the darkness as he could not help himself see the bright side of life. Amber was so hungry for love and adventure and a young man who could make her feel a desired woman again. She was doing everything she could to keep their relationship. David needed financial help, and Amber became his provider.

David promised the sky to Amber, and Amber hoped with him, but the reality was another thing. He thought that women only liked sex and heavy metal music. David was trying to behave with Amber as if she were an immature young girl, but although Amber looked very young for her age, she was a mature, sexy woman. After one month together, she started understanding what his actions meant. Amber was feeling very involved and more attached to him by his personal stories, and that made him get back to his artistic and creative side. He got back to drawing, painting, and making anything out of recycled objects, and that impressed Amber. He was happier. He became dependent on Amber's words of affection, and his obsession grew stronger to the point that he once said convincingly, 'You are my life, Amber, and without you, I do not want to live.' This caused worry in Amber's mind as she did not want that. There was nothing she could do but say to him, 'Dear David, I will always be with you. If it is not as your woman, it will be as your friend,' but he responded, 'No, my love, I want you to be with me as my wife and the bearer of my children.'

Amber was pleased to have heard these words. However, she knew that she could not bear children, and she thought everything was moving too fast. Amber said to David, 'Let fate take its course as we cannot run before we can walk.' David and Amber were connected by fate.

On the other hand, Amber faced the town and her family's prejudices. They could not comprehend what Amber was trying to do with David as she was still a married woman. She was determined to help him and enjoy their time together. David became less offensive to people. Amber spoke to David about her niece; he confidently said that he had no interest in her, so Amber felt reassured. David tried to do his best to convince Amber of his love for her, but she started to feel that he did not really love her. Amber realised that on the day they were walking in a nearby town with busy streets and lots of traffic. David kept on walking ahead of her even though he knew that Amber was not used to the area. He seemed to prefer to walk on his own as if he did not know Amber and as if he had something to hide and did not want to be seen walking with her. Amber decided to stop as he was too far ahead, and she turned back and kept on walking the opposite way.

David realised that she was not behind him, so he ran back towards her and asked her, 'What are you doing?'

Amber told him, 'I just want to go home,' and David said, 'That is okay. Let's go home.' Amber replied convincingly, 'I mean I am going home to my family.' At that moment, all Amber thought was how Joel looked after her, and she realised that she still had feelings for Joel. Joel's only fault was his gambling habit. Her love for David was more of a hiding place, somewhere she could listen to words she wanted to hear. Also, she could talk about art and many other subjects as David seemed to love reading and had lots of knowledge about books. At the beginning, the relationship between Amber and David was full of love and tenderness, but a few months later, reality struck—David told Amber he could not work and Amber was to provide the money for his needs. It was a cruel reality, but Amber was facing it.

Rose opened her eyes to find her darling love, James, listening to her story, drying her tears. 'My darling James,' she said sweetly, 'you have me, and I will always be with you through time. I wish you could come to my world and stay with me.'

James responded, 'Darling, I would love to.'

'My darling James, it is amazing how life changes the way you see certain situations. Now I want to stay here with you and forget all about that world. I think of my lovely family, but they are used to being without me. Shall I continue with my story about David, darling?' asked Rose tenderly and relaxed.

'Yes, my darling, please continue,' James replied.

Rose told James that she continued seeing David, her warrior, as she used to call him. She wanted David to feel strong and positive. She followed his game. David's aim was to make old Amber feel loved; that was his speciality. Amber was aware of everything that was happening. Her feelings towards David changed. Amber knew that David's love was more towards her niece and that she was nothing but a mere convenience to David. At this moment, Amber could not stop thinking about Joel and his loyalty.

Amber found herself at her mother's garden in South America, outside her bedroom, remembering herself telling the story about David to James. It was a sunny day, and she was feeling some kind of tranquillity. All of a sudden, the phone rang, and it was David. He wanted to know where she was and the reason she had not turned up for the past few days. Amber told him that she was needed at home to look after her mother as she did not want to tell him directly about her changed feelings towards him. Using his sweet talk and charming ways, he pleaded her to come back and stay with him, but this time, his words did not reach Amber's heart. Despite all this, Amber tried very hard not to hurt his feelings, so she reassured him that she would see him the following day.

A month later, Rose appeared once again in the park, having suffered a flashback about her lying unconscious in a hospital in South America. She looked around, and James was not there. That was unusual; she was worried and went to his house. She knocked on the door, and a nurse came out. 'How may I help?' she asked abruptly. She was tall, had fair skin and a good figure but was arrogant. She looked at Rose as if she were an enemy. Rose asked for James, and she told her he was asleep.

'Please, madam, I need to see him,' Rose pleaded.

'Are you his acquaintance?' asked the nurse.

'Yes, I am,' Rose replied softly.

'Would you please come in, but you should wait until it is time for his medication.'

Rose's eyes were full of tears. That was what made the nurse feel pity for her, and she became softer. Rose went to the sitting room and sat down. 'When is the medication due?' asked Rose sweetly.

'I should wake him up in one hour, madam,' the nurse replied.

The hour passed, and the nurse woke up James to give him the medicine and told him about Rose. James was feeling weak, but a smile showed up on his pale face. He said pleadingly, 'Please, Ms Laurens, ask her to come and see me.'

Rose heard him and ran to his bedside. 'Oh, James, my darling, what happened? How did you get like this? Is it okay for you to talk?' said Rose anxiously.

'My darling Rose, you are my medicine. I feel better already. I am delighted to see you. You have been away for so long, my darling, and I was missing you so much. Louise died three weeks ago, and little James is with my parents in Surrey Manor. I feel guilty for not loving her as much as she did love me. Please, darling, make me some of your nice tea.'

Rose went to make the tea, and Ms Laurens said to Rose, 'I am glad you have come. He seems to be in better spirits. Please stay with him. He seems to need you.' Rose stayed with him overnight, lying by his side. As James started recuperating, the nurse was able to take a time off, and they had the house for themselves. They lived their moments as if they were the last. James said to Rose, 'My darling Rose, I love you, and even if you are in love with David, this is our world, and he is not part of it. Rose looked at him sweetly and asked him not to get too excited as he had not yet recovered, and he calmed down and kissed her lips softly.

'Darling, I want to know what happened to you. Tell me, my darling, please,' repeated Rose, but James was too tired and fell asleep with his hand holding hers.

When he woke up, he looked for Rose, and there she was, sleeping by his side. He felt very reassured and overjoyed as she had not disappeared. She stayed with him. He kissed her cheek softly and let her sleep. The following day, James was up early and brought Rose breakfast. She woke up and looked at him, smiling.

'Sorry, my darling,' Rose said, 'I overslept. I am supposed to be looking after you, and now you are looking after me. If the nurse sees this, she is going to be angry with me. Come and sit by my side, darling.'

The nurse came in the morning, gave him the medicines, and felt very happy to see him up and about. 'I do not think you need me any more, Mr James,' she said convincingly.

He smiled pleasantly. 'I think that I still need you, Ms Laurens. I am afraid Rose might need to go, we never know.' James and Rose both looked at each other. James's dream was to have Rose with him forever. 'No one could replace you, Rose. You will always be my Rose,' he said sweetly and sadly. 'Rose darling, would you like to stay with me forever?'

Rose thought about David and Joel and felt herself attached to the three of them. 'My darling James, you and I have been honest with each other, and you know I would love to stay here with you, but part of my life is with them in the other world. If we stay as it is, I am happy, and I wish you to be happy too.'

James looked at her sweetly and said, 'As long as you always come back to me, it will be fine.'

'I promise, I will always come back to you, my darling,' said Rose. 'I have been thinking about Joel.'

'Why, darling?' asked James.

'Because I am now sure I still have feelings for him.'

'My darling Rose,' said James sweetly, 'I love you very much with all my heart, and being your confidant makes me the proudest lover and friend, and nothing will change ever.'

Rose said, 'Thank you, darling.'

'I know David was feeling too much loneliness at his age. He did not know how to keep a woman as you do, my darling. He needed to find a way to escape, and he found Amber to play with.'

'My darling,' said James, 'David needed to learn his lesson. You are an angel who got her wings broken when he threw you for another one, and he should have been more caring. He did not know that Amber loved him dearly and would do anything for him. And this new angel is beautiful but her heart is with someone else.'

Rose was feeling happier in an unusual way as if nothing was to worry her any more. It was a strange sensation that made her feel mysteriously cold and made her remember the old man.

'Tell me, my darling, are there any more developments in your other life? You have me so interested,' said James after kissing and making love to Rose. She sat on the bed, looking at him with tenderness, and said, 'Darling James, I am scared but happy.'

'Why is that?' James asked Rose.

'David seemed determined to make me happy. He asked me to forget the past and start again.'

'Did you believe him, darling? Be honest!' asked James.

'Darling, honestly, I did not believe him. It was difficult to trust again,' said Rose.

'I do not blame you, darling. On the contrary, I am very proud of you,' said James.

'Darling James, David behaved the way he did because of strong reasons, and they could have happened when he was a boy. We could understand him better if we knew more about him,' Rose said convincingly. 'I feel something strange, darling James. I feel extremely relaxed now that David is in the past and I do not have to worry about him any more. Also, I feel I wish I could get back to Joel, but it seems it cannot happen.'

'Well, what you feel is rather extraordinary, darling, as you have been appearing in and disappearing from this town due to your worries.'

'I do not feel worried any more, darling,' said Rose calmly.

'Darling, have you realised that you have been recollecting about David and Joel and you have not disappeared again? It is rather out of the ordinary, but it makes me feel very happy,' said James, pleased.

'Not sure what is happening, but if I can stay here longer, I will be very happy. You will help me not to miss them, won't you, darling?' Rose asked tenderly.

'My darling, you know that our relationship is a special one and there is no space for envy, obsession, intrigues, or misunderstandings. We are one, darling.'

'I love you, my darling, and you know that I love Joel and David. Perhaps I was asking for the type of love that they could not give me and the type of love you could not give to Louise, may God bless her,' said Rose.

'By the way, darling, we have been invited to Loren and Paul's wedding!' James said enthusiastically.

'I am so happy for them, darling,' said Rose. When Rose said those words, at the same time, Joel was thinking about Amber, his sweet wife, who was in South America. He was patiently waiting for her.

David's Nightmare

David was born in a little town called Guayaba in South America. The town had one Christian church, and opposite was a small round park with the statue of Simón Bolívar in its centre. Also, there were palm trees and oak trees around the park, and there were quite a few benches, which people used to sit while enjoying the fresh air. Sundays used to be the busiest day, and people enjoyed the friendly atmosphere. There was also a foreign factory that helped the town's progress. Each year, the town looked better, and there were jobs for the community.

David was the only boy among four sisters. Through his childhood, he had been a little nervous as he had a problem in his throat. It seemed to be too tight; therefore, feeding was a struggle. He would choke easily, so on a few occasions, he almost encountered death.

David was his grandma's favourite grandson. He was slim with lovely olive skin and wavy dark hair; he looked like an Indian warrior. His grandmother loved him more than her other grandsons, and he corresponded to such maternal love. She used to take him everywhere she went and used to buy him clothes and presents. David showed his gratefulness by being the best in school. It was due to his grandma's love and protection what made him feel happy and secured.

When he was six years old, he was pretty advanced in his learning, and his teacher was amazed at his rapid progress. David felt so proud of himself, and he knew his grandma felt it too. His grandma died when he was nine years of age, and that was a big blow for David as he had loved her dearly. From that day on, David became withdrawn and a loner. In spite of enjoying learning, he started seeing school as a prison. He felt insecure and uncomfortable at school. He was a very calm little boy, eager to acquire academic knowledge, and this awoke the anger of his classmates to the point that they started to torture him and make him feel miserable and lonely.

The lady teacher used to use David as an example of good behaviour in front of his classmates, but this caused more problems to him. The calm little boy became the terrorised one. They bullied him so much. David was always quiet and ready to receive the physical and mental ill treatments, and it was too much to bear.

There was no one to defend him and no one to talk about it with. His sisters were in a school near to his, but they could not do anything to help. His classmates began to cause trouble in school and put the blame on him. This made his teachers, who had never questioned him before, angry at him. They punished him, leaving the real responsible ones free of punishment. That was the time when David was crying out silently for help. He felt sentenced to suffer. He questioned himself as to why his classmates hit him so badly just because he was different.

David questioned his existence as he did not understand why these things were happening to him. He felt indignant. That was his life, and he had to live it. His situation continued until he finished his primary school when he was eleven. He did not want to be the best student any more as he thought being good did not pay off. He was in an unbearable moment of desperation. David's father worked in the factory, but due to his alcoholic addiction and his attraction to women and pleasure, his son was not part of his life when he most needed him.

At the age of thirteen, he felt himself different, excluded from society. He started feeling cruelty from people. He became difficult to talk to, and vulgarity was his main way of showing his internal anger. He started getting immersed in his own world, believing in the dark side of life. A friend introduced him to heavy metal music, and he identified himself with it. He became very irritating to everyone; that was his way of showing off and catching people's attention.

His father became his enemy; his mother became a sad woman who suffered from his behaviour. Not knowing what to do, she decided to take the children and leave her husband. She went to a faraway town, not knowing it was a red zone controlled by various rebel groups. During this period, David and his sisters witnessed some horrific scenes of death and mutilation at such a young age, which caused them so much trauma to the point that the government took them out together with other families and placed them in different neighbouring towns where it was safer to live. They returned to the town and lived in his father's house.

He started living a double life between good and evil, a bit like Dr Jekyll and Mr Hyde, but in reality, he wanted a good change in his life. He continued living without positive motivation for years. His love for art was one of his ways of escaping from reality, and he focused on Gothic art. His room was painted black, and he drew skeletons and satanic symbols. One day, when he was working as a builder, he fell on his back. More anger rose in him as he thought he was unlucky. The back pain was intense, and it added to his eating problems, which became more of a burden for him. Deep inside, he was crying out to be saved, to be taken out from darkness, but the heavy metal ideology was a place where he could hide and take all his anger out. It became his shell.

Ball of Fire

David was moved to a new school, where he performed much better. He was happier, but due to financial problems, his parents decided to enrol him in the old school once again. This time, David was stronger, and he claimed respect from his classmates. He had decided that whoever tried to hit him would receive a hit back. He became confident and strong, a bit too much for his age. Years passed, and David became a terror; he was so angry and in pain. Every time David went out with his friends, his family never knew his whereabouts.

One evening, on his way back home, he found an old art book lying on the road. He picked it up and took it with him. Just before he went to sleep, he read a few pages, and that night, David had a strange dream which he did not tell anybody about.

In the dream, David found himself in a palace, and there was this lovely girl who looked like a princess. She was seated on a throne, crying. David was looking at her but could not talk to her. She was talking aloud. 'Anthony, my warrior, my love, why can we not be together? Why is destiny against us? Where did they take you, my love? Why can I not find you? Why?' she continued saying and crying. David could not recognise the name Anthony. As soon as the princess's mother made her entrance, David woke up and thought about the dream and the lovely princess.

The dream got him preoccupied; he felt as if the princess were crying for him, but he could not understand why. He did not speak about his dream to anybody.

When David reached his thirties, he still physically appeared like in his twenties. He was into his heavy metal world. He was looking for love, but he only found frustration as he did not know how to give it. Despite David's gallantry and lovemaking skills, he was in and out of relationships frequently. This situation made him angrier as he could not find true love. He was tired of one-night stands. He was submerged in the darkness of his heavy metal world for years, so he became very vindictive.

One day, he picked a beautiful young girl in her teens. Together with his heavy metal friends, he decided to make a plan on how to abduct her and play all sort of games with her. She belonged to a family he hated in the town. She was a Christian follower, and he felt himself a Satan follower. He thought, *This will be my time to taste such a lovely body and do everything I want.* Listening to the dark heavy metal music made him feel more aggressive, and he enjoyed it.

One night, once again, David had another dream with the princess. She was talking to an old man who seemed to be a wizard. He was tall and with a long white beard, and he was carrying a stick.

The wizard was saying to her, 'My princess Anytha, do not be sad. Fate has been your enemy. You fell in love with someone different from your caste and background. The warrior loves you deeply and will always do. As love is the greatest feeling a human can have, I am going to cast a spell on you.'

The princess was in such a state of sadness. Raising her eyes to the old man, she asked, 'What spell?' She had the hope to meet her lover, her warrior of love, as she used to call him. Suddenly the old man raised his stick and said, 'You will be together with your love in the timeless zone once he passes the test of love.' Princess Anytha did not understand at that time what the spell was about.

As usual, Anthony, the warrior, met the princess in their hidden garden, but on this particular day, he asked her to run away with him. She responded negatively despite her love for Anthony. One part of her wanted to leave with Anthony, but the other part could not allow her to disrespect her loving family. As Anthony could not accept her negative response, he became furious and asked her to forget about him as he was to forget about her. Anthony said that it was the last time they would meet up as she had chosen to stay with her parents.

Princess Anytha suffered in silence. She could not believe what she was hearing. *Anthony's love was a lie, and how could he forget me so easily?* she thought. She walked back to the palace; no good farewell was said. Days passed by. The princess was feeling lonelier, and her love for Anthony grew deeper. A few months later, she became terribly ill. Anthony had disappeared, no sign of him. The physician was called to the palace, and he could not find what the cause of the princess's illness was. He saw her weak and unable to speak. Only when she pronounced the words *the wizard*, the king and queen immediately sent for him as their only hope to get their child back.

The wizard went to see her and talked to her about her warrior. He said to her that they were to be together no matter what, and in spite of being so ill and so weak, she managed to smile and died peacefully. Suddenly someone was shouting and trying to get into the palace, and that was Anthony. He wanted to see the princess, but the wizard told him that it was too late as she had already died. Anthony ran to her bedside and kissed her, trying to revive her. His pain was the deepest. He was asking her for forgiveness.

Months passed by, and Anthony's anger was growing. He could not find peace. He could not accept Anytha's death. Anthony's mother became very worried about him, so she went to see the wizard, begging him to help her son as she knew there was a spell. The wizard thought about it and asked the mother to ask Anthony to go and see him.

The wizard said to him, 'Anthony, as you know, I cast a spell on you and Anytha before she died, and she knows she will be waiting for you through eternity. To meet her again, you have to pass a test of love. It is going to be a hard one, but if you really want to be with her, you will pass it. You will have to find a human who can love and feel real love for his lover, and when you have succeeded, you will see the princess asking you to hold her hand, and you will be together forever.'

Anthony told the wizard, 'It is not a hard one. I will find such a man. I will get my princess back,' and he went like a ball of fire through distance and time. David woke up from his dream and thought, *This is so real.* He still did not care about it, but he realised something strange had happened to him.

The following night, he went to his room and fell asleep. His room was dark, and the only shapes that could be seen were the white skeletons he had painted on the wall. Suddenly he was awakened by a humming sound, and he could see on the wall a bright point that became bigger and bigger each time. A ball of fire emerged, taking over his room, and David felt very scared until a warrior from ancient Egypt appeared through the wall. David thought it was a dream. He liked it as darkness and mystery was his favourite theme. He decided to enjoy such a dream. Gradually he started feeling happier as if he were watching a film on TV, but he did not know what was in store for him.

Suddenly the ancient warrior spoke arrogantly to him, 'David, you have been chosen.' David still could not believe it was part of reality and kept quiet. 'You have been invoking souls, and I heard you. I have a mission for you, and you have no choice but to accomplish it.' The warrior was laughing loudly, and David said, 'Stop laughing, you will wake up my mother.' Anthony laughed and said, 'Good! Now that you can hear me, listen carefully. From now on, you and I will be one.' David thought this was a prank someone was playing on him. The warrior started turning so fast and became a ball of fire and went inside David. David lost consciousness and fell asleep.

From that moment, David's life changed. He felt as if he were another person, newly born. David was not scared any more. Anthony started to talk to David in his sleep, ordering him to fall in love with whoever passed his way. It was easy for Anthony to get into his body as David was weak. Now David was Anthony's slave.

One morning, David was feeling strong and energetic. He felt he had a mission. Anthony was now part of David's life, and he did not know it was his reality. David started having nightmares every night. It was Anthony's memories of fights, and that triggered

David's memories of the killings he witnessed. Also, he could see the princess again. They were meeting in a beautiful garden. David was experiencing these meetings every night. He thought he was in love with the princess. He remembered how they had met in hidden gardens as the king, her father, and the queen did not accept him as her match. He was a warrior, and they wanted a prince. Anthony and Anytha loved each other immensely and promised eternal love.

David used to get up in the morning and drew images of what he dreamt. He was feeling happy and in love. He started having relationships with married women as the young ones did not fall into his sex games. He was submerged deeper into darkness, heavy metal music, alcohol, fights, and breaking women's hearts, which were Anthony's pleasures. Every woman who passed by was enchanted by David. The years passed by, but David could not fall in love with any woman, and he felt it was not right. He had to fight with Anthony. David wanted to spend his time doing art, but Anthony would get him out of the house at any time. David was feeling achy, sick, and lonely every day.

Anthony said to David, 'You are so weak, David. You must show me that you can love as much as I love my princess.' David was confused as he knew about the princess. He could not believe that Anthony knew the same princess that he saw in his dreams.

David's body could not resist Anthony's type of life. The long heavy metal concerts had made a mess psychologically on David's mind. He was feeling so scared of heights; big buildings were like monsters ready to attack him. He preferred to be home. Anthony could not give up his mission, so he decided to push David to complete it.

There she was—Vicky, the lovely brunette who lived in the town. Anthony was infatuated with her too, so through David, Anthony started writing messages to Vicky. She never answered, but he could feel she loved his words 'my lovely princess' and 'the most beautiful among the beauties'. David was happy trying to conquer her until one day Amber appeared in the picture.

David loved Amber in his own way, and he found in her a great companion. She could love him. She could care and help him to get out of the darkness and take him away from Anthony. Vicky knew nothing about David and Anthony. David did not want Anthony to hurt Vicky. He thought Vicky was an angel, sweet and pure, so he would keep her safe. Amber was an older and stronger woman; he felt some kind of protection from her, so David decided to go for Amber.

David used all the necessary techniques to conquer Amber. He became a great lover and a companion. She was able to understand him like no one could. Anthony was the happiest as he thought that was the opportunity he was waiting for to fulfil his mission to get him to his princess.

David used the most loving and romantic words when addressing Amber, and she melted under his enchanting manners. David got so attached to her that he knew no one could take her place. She cared so much for him that she forgot Joel and the man in her dream, James. She was for him and no one else. Their meetings were passionate, and their promises about love and eternity were their favourite subject. They were extremely involved in each other, and nothing else seemed to move around them.

David promised Amber she was his only love, but with time, Amber started to realise that David was infatuated with Vicky. He was fighting with himself and his real feelings. One day, David and Vicky met on the street, and they exchanged glances and smiles like two lovers. David did not realise that Amber was watching them. Amber was in such a shock; she seemed to be in agony, so she got to David's house and directed herself to the backyard. It was raining heavily. She was devastated and wanted to die. She saw the big lemon tree and cuddled it, crying. Her heart was so weak that it could not beat any more.

David rushed home and asked for Amber's whereabouts. He was told that she was in the backyard. He thought about what she could be doing out there in the rain.

He rushed to her, and when he saw her body lying on the ground, he could not believe it. It was Amber's body, and he just fell to pieces. Anthony was happy as he started seeing his princess Anytha coming from a distance, offering her hand as the wizard had said. David was desolated, and his heart was rapidly palpitating.

When he held Amber's face, he thought she was dead but did not realise she had just passed out; she was in a state of coma. David cried until his body did not respond. He died embracing her. Suddenly David's mother appeared and called for help as she saw them flat under the tree. David's dead body lay next to Amber's. At that moment, Anthony's soul started getting out of David's body and said, 'David, I did not have the time to thank you for helping me. I know it was not your choice, but you were good. I am sorry you did not get your princess, but I hope you get your queen in eternity.' Anytha, the princess, was calling Anthony again. 'My warrior, my love, together forever,' she said, whispering. They walked through eternity, cuddling each other, followed by the old wizard, and vanished.

David's soul was left alone walking through eternity, waiting for the wizard's promise to come back for him. People in South America mourned the loss of David. Amber was taken to a hospital, where she recovered few weeks later. She was told what happened to David so, she went to the cemetery for a last farewell. Then, She decided to get back to London, hoping to meet Joel and expecting he had dealt with his gambling addiction. Also, she remembered James and their extraordinary relationship. Despite the beauty of her dream, Amber was still in need of real love. While on the plane, Amber could not stop thinking about how life or destiny had taken her away from her principles and real love to the unknown.

THE OLD MAN

Back in the eighteenth century in Egypt, in a little town near Cairo, a woman called Lilly from a well-off family was having a very stressful time. Her husband had other wives, and she had become next to nothing in his heart. She was so desperate, living in a small town full of prejudices and old traditions. Her desires to be happy and be of some importance to her husband were like drops of water to a thirsty soul. She loved him dearly and wanted him to be like he was when they had first met.

One day, she was walking through the market in Cairo when she saw an old man waving and inviting her to his stall. He was selling old souvenirs that looked old and tatty.

'Salaam!' she said to the old man, and he replied, 'Alaikum salaam.'

'Do you want to speak to me? Or sell me one of your worn-out items?' asked Lilly courteously. The old man half smiled and said, 'As the saying goes, never judge a book by its cover, madam. I was told to call you over.'

So she asked him, 'Who asked you to do so?'

'This feather,' said the old man as he picked it up from the stall and showed it to her.

Lilly could not believe what the man was saying, but she was sure the man did not mean to cause any harm. 'And what else has the feather said?' asked Lilly inquisitively.

The old man said, 'You have been chosen.'

'What have I been chosen for?' asked Lilly, surprised.

'My dear Lilly . . .' Confusion registered on her face for she had not told the old man her name. The old man continued, 'I only follow instructions, and I need to give you this feather and beg you to look after it. Please keep it in a safe place. It augurs good times for you.'

Lilly got distracted by the other sellers in the marketplace as the normal arguments and thieves were stirring the atmosphere. When she looked back at the old man's stall, it was no longer there; it had vanished. She looked around but could not find a trace. *Well, that was all very strange*, she thought.

While this was happening, a woman had been observing Lilly talking to the old man and was interested in what they talked about. She was a maid. Having been brought up in a strict religious Muslim household, she thought herself virtuous, but deep inside she could feel envious and jealous about anything. She wanted the feather badly. She got distracted and did not see where Lilly went, so she decided to continue visiting the market until she could see her again.

Since Lilly had the feather, she became liberated and peaceful. No negative feelings any more, and she became a happy woman. Once again, she was walking along the market, and Amina, the maid, approached her and tried to establish some rapport.

'Salaam,' Amina said to Lilly.

'Alaikum salaam,' responded Lilly.

'My lady,' said Amina, 'can I ask you where you bought your sarong? It is so beautiful and special.'

'Thanks, madam,' answered Lilly and told her that she had bought it from a merchant in the market the previous year. Amina helped her carry her groceries, so a friendship was born. Lilly trusted her, but Amina had her own plans.

One day, Lilly invited Amina to her house for a cup of green tea, and that was the opportunity Amina had been waiting for. The moment Lilly left for the kitchen to prepare the tea, Amina took advantage of Lilly's absence and sneaked into her bedroom to look for the feather and found it in her chest drawer. She slyly took it and rapidly hid it under her garments. When Lilly got back, Amina was on her way out, excusing herself as she needed to go home urgently.

When Amina got to her house, she observed the feather and could not see anything special about it. It did not shine as she had seen it the first time when the old man gave it to Lilly. That night, when she was asleep, she was awakened by a loud voice demanding her to return the feather to the rightful owner; otherwise, she was to be cursed. She thought it was just a dream, so she ignored it. Since then, Amina carried on having the most terrifying nightmares. She got so scared about them and decided to take the feather back.

Amina decided to see Lilly and knocked on her door. Lilly opened the door and invited her in for a drink. The first chance Amina was left alone, she ran to Lilly's bedroom and placed the feather back where she found it. She felt relieved and relaxed. She got back to the living room as Lilly was coming with hot tea. Lilly said to Amina, 'Thanks for coming and returning the feather.' Amina, with great astonishment, said, 'I have not taken anything from here, Lilly. You are misjudging me!' Lilly said calmly, 'It is fine, Amina. It was just your curiosity.'

Time passed by, and when Lilly died of old age, Amina went to Lilly's house and looked slyly for the feather once again but to no avail as the feather had vanished. Lilly's sons told the people in the town that their mother had died peacefully.

Also, one of Lilly's sons told them that the night his mother died, he had seen in the house, among the mourners, an old man he had never seen before. He saw him enter the room, and then he did not see him going out. When he looked through the window, he saw a golden bird in the distance. 'The Egyptian phoenix, the bird of love and peace!' a group of mourners exclaimed excitedly.

Lightning Source UK Ltd.
Milton Keynes UK
UKOW02f0832220116

266906UK00001B/27/P